Wh
at

"R.J. Patterson does a fantastic job at keeping you engaged and interested. I look forward to more from this talented author."

- Aaron Patterson
bestselling author of SWEET DREAMS

DEAD SHOT

"Small town life in southern Idaho might seem quaint and idyllic to some. But when local newspaper reporter Cal Murphy begins to uncover a series of strange deaths that are linked to a sticky spider web of deception, the lid on the peaceful town is blown wide open. Told with all the energy and bravado of an old pro, first-timer R.J. Patterson hits one out of the park his first time at bat with *Dead Shot*. It's that good."

- Vincent Zandri
bestselling author of THE REMAINS

"You can tell R.J. knows what it's like to live in the newspaper world, but with *Dead Shot*, he's proven that he also can write one heck of a murder mystery."

- Josh Katzowitz
NFL writer for CBSSports.com
& author of Sid Gillman: Father of the Passing Game

"Patterson has a mean streak about a mile wide and puts his two main characters through quite a horrible ride, which makes for good reading."

- Richard D., reader

DEAD LINE

"This book kept me on the edge of my seat the whole time. I didn't really want to put it down. R.J. Patterson has hooked me. I'll be back for more."

- Bob Behler
3-time Idaho broadcaster of the year
and play-by-play voice for Boise State football

"Like a John Grisham novel, from the very start I was pulled right into the story and couldn't put the book down. It was as if I personally knew and cared about what happened to each of the main characters. Every chapter ended with so much excitement and suspense I had to continue to read until I learned how it ended, even though it kept me up until 3:00 A.M.

- Ray F., reader

DEAD IN THE WATER

"In Dead in the Water, R.J. Patterson accurately captures the action-packed saga of a what could be a real-life college football scandal. The sordid details will leave readers flipping through the pages as fast as a hurry-up offense."

- Mark Schlabach,
ESPN college sports columnist and
co-author of *Called to Coach*
and *Heisman: The Man Behind the Trophy*

THE WARREN OMISSIONS

"What can be more fascinating than a super high concept novel that reopens the conspiracy behind the JFK assassination while the threat of a global world war rests in the balance? With his new novel, *The Warren Omissions*, former journalist turned bestselling author R.J. Patterson proves he just might be the next worthy successor to Vince Flynn."

- Vincent Zandri
bestselling author of THE REMAINS

TWO MINUTES TO MIDNIGHT

A Brady Hawk novel

R.J. PATTERSON

TWO MINUTES TO MIDNIGHT
© Copyright 2018 R.J. Patterson

First Print Edition 2018

Cover Design by Books Covered

Published in the United States of America
Green E-Books
Boise Idaho 83713

*For Lee Harter, for teaching me
what it meant to be a journalist*

CHAPTER 1

Kensington, London

LIAM DAVENPORT STOOD on the front porch of his home and looked skyward as the ominous clouds gathered over the London sky. He checked in both directions down the street, searching for anything out of the ordinary. With a background in reconnaissance while serving in the British Army, he couldn't escape the habit of surveying every detail. That instinct had worked well for him since he was selected as the Secretary of State for Defense. His knack for maneuvering through impossible situations enabled him to guide the British military through one of the most dangerous eras in modern warfare. The physical landscape was just as fraught with landmines as was the political backdrop. Yet Davenport had a keen eye for navigating to safety by finding the best exit strategies. However, if the meteorologists were to be believed, only an act of God could save them from the remnants of Hurricane Thomas that had chugged across the Atlantic. Downgraded to nothing more than a weak tropical storm, it was in search of a place to unleash its final punch.

"Papa, are you going to come inside soon?" asked Millie, his spunky eight-year-old daughter. "Benjamin wants to play another round of Qwirkle."

Davenport scanned the area once more before taking a deep breath and turning around to face Millie.

"I suppose I should come inside," he said. "There's nothing I can do out here, worrying about the weather."

He followed Millie into the house and spun to shut the door. But the wind grabbed it, slamming it shut and rattling the windows.

Ava, his twelve-year-old bookworm, glanced up from her novel and shot her father a look. "Upset that you can't control the weather, too?"

Davenport shook his head subtly and chose not to respond. His eldest daughter was still upset over the confiscation of her smartphone after sending racy pictures to one of her classmates. He was bewildered by such behavior, let alone that his daughter thought she could escape his watchful eye.

The television was on as a report detailed the story of several bodies found floating in the Thames.

With a somber expression, the newscaster spoke as footage showed the dead face down, rocking along the choppy water. He warned viewers about the danger of being near the edge of the river, explaining how occasional gusts observed by meteorologists topped eighty miles per hour with sustained winds of more than fifty.

"This is not the time to be daring. This is the time to be wise and stay indoors at all costs."

Davenport clucked his tongue. "Let's turn off the tele. I've had enough depressing news for one day."

The family cat, Mr. Muggles, eased up to Davenport, rubbing against his leg. Davenport scooped the cat up and scratched his head, resulting in a satisfied purr.

"I hear someone wants to lose another game of Qwirkle," Davenport announced.

Benjamin, who had been busily gathering all the game tiles and shoving them back into the grab bag, wore a ear-to-ear grin as he looked up at his father. "Another game?" Benjamin asked. "I haven't lost the first one yet."

Davenport took his seat at the head of the table next to Benjamin and was quickly joined by Millie and his wife, Evelyn.

"Six tiles each," Benjamin reminded everyone has he reached into the bag.

A loud crack against the side of the house arrested everyone's attention, even Ava's as she looked up from her book.

"What was that?" she asked.

Davenport looked around the table at his family, all wide-eyed with fear.

"I'll take a look," he said as he stood and wandered over to the window.

He turned the back porch light on and identified the culprit. A broken branch was lying on the ground.

"Just a branch," he said. "Nothing to worry about."

"What if one of those branches comes flying through our window?" Ava asked.

"Then we'll clean it up and patch up the window," Davenport said. "There's nothing we can do about it except wait for the storm to pass."

A half hour later, the power went out, resulting in a collective moan from the game players and a mini tantrum from Ava about how she couldn't finish the book now. Benjamin jumped up from the table and raced over to the junk drawer in the adjacent kitchen. He rummaged through their collection of random items until he found a lighter and a pair of votive candles.

"Think this will be enough light for us to finish the game?" Benjamin asked.

Davenport glanced at his watch. "It's actually getting late. Why don't we just call it a night and get ready for bed?"

His suggestion was met with immediate rejection by Millie and Benjamin.

"You just don't want to lose," Millie said.

"There's plenty of time for a comeback," Davenport said. "But it's getting close to your bedtime. Besides, the best way to ride out a storm like this is asleep in a bed."

None of his children liked the idea, but they didn't protest any more. They knew better than to push their father more than once.

A loud knock at the door made everyone pause as all eyes went to Davenport.

"I'll handle it," he said. "I'm sure it's nothing."

"Who could be calling on us this late on a Sunday evening?" Evelyn asked.

Davenport stood. "I'll answer it," he said as he strode across the room.

He stopped before opening the door and glanced back over his shoulder at the rest of his family, who were all frozen as they awaited the revelation of the mystery guest.

"Well, go on," Davenport said. "Get ready for bed. I'm sure this doesn't concern you."

He turned back toward the door and twisted the

knob. On the front step was Col. Thomas Lloyd, who was struggling to keep his cap on top of his head.

"We need to talk, sir," Lloyd said, squinting as the rain blew sideways and pelted him in the face.

"Want to come in?" Davenport asked, gesturing inside his house.

Lloyd peered behind Davenport. "It's probably best that you stepped outside here with me. It'll only take a minute."

Davenport furrowed his brow and pulled the door shut behind him as he joined Lloyd on the porch.

"What could possibly be happening that forced you to pay me a visit at my home?"

"I'm sorry, sir," Lloyd said. "But it'll all make sense when I give you a full briefing."

"Go on."

"Marshall Hampton from the joint task force overseeing our operation to infiltrate radical terrorist cells just delivered some disconcerting news regarding all the bodies found floating in the Thames earlier this evening."

Davenport scowled. "Those weren't just foolish kids?"

Lloyd shook his head. "Those were some of our best agents who had been deeply embedded in various cells. Some of those agents had been working under-cover for as long as seven years."

"And like that," Davenport said, snapping his fingers, "they show back up in London, dead in the Thames?"

"Yes, and this wasn't just one particular cell. By Hampton's count, these were agents working inside a half dozen cells. One was in the Congo, another in Somalia, and the other four were in the Middle East. They were from all over."

"Looks like someone planted the bodies there to get our attention."

"They got what they wanted, whoever *they* is," Lloyd said.

Davenport looked up at the streetlight as the wind continued to push the rain horizontally along the road. "How could anyone learn the identities of these agents? That information isn't easily accessible even through our own computer system."

"Hampton believes this is linked back to the Black Wolf hack a couple years ago."

"But Black Wolf's computer equipment and files were all seized. And didn't he end up dead?"

"Apparently that was all staged. Nobody knew his true identity."

"So you're saying Black Wolf is still alive?" Davenport asked.

"Either that or someone managed to get their hands on the list of agents he extracted when he hacked into our database."

Davenport let fly a few expletives before he stared pensively out at the street. "Hampton's agents were the ones feeding us intel on how to target our strikes."

"I know, sir. Calling it a tremendous setback feels like an understatement."

"Does Hampton have a plan?"

"That's what he wants to talk with you about. We need to figure out a way to move forward because right now we're flying blind out there."

Davenport sighed. "Let me get my coat. I have a feeling it's going to be a long night."

CHAPTER 2

Kauai, Hawaii

HAWK SKIDDED TO A STOP on his mountain bike atop a cliff overlooking the South Pacific Ocean. It had been far too long since he had last stopped to enjoy sunny blue skies while exploring a breath-taking scene in nature. And drinking it all in with Alex made the moment that much more special.

Alex slammed on her brakes and sprayed dirt all over Hawk's bike and legs.

"I didn't know this was a race," she said as she narrowed her eyes. "What happened to stopping and smelling the roses?"

"What do you think this is?" Hawk asked as he gestured toward the sprawling landscape. "I'm stopped, and I'm smelling."

"You're smelling," she said, cracking a faint smile, "but it's nothing like roses. More like a mix of gym socks and garlic."

"Biting your tongue isn't your thing, is it?" Hawk asked.

"Are you just now figuring that out?"

Hawk flashed a wry grin and jerked his bike in the opposite direction. "Race you to the next peak."

Without hesitating, he started pedaling, churning along the path. He could still hear Alex's griping about how unfair it was above his wheels slicing through the soft sand.

Hawk pumped hard and glanced back over his shoulder at Alex. He knew how she would take the act of leaving her in the dust, but he was hoping she'd forgive him once she figured out why.

Once Hawk reached the next overlook point, he signaled to the three men who were waiting for him. They shuffled back behind the bushes and brought out a small table, covered with a gourmet dinner for two. Hawk helped them set a pair of chairs in place before everyone took their positions.

Alex was grumbling with her head down as she reached the plateau. With only a slight glance up, she hadn't fully taken in the scene before her.

"I swear, Hawk, you act like you're some chivalrous gentleman, but I'm beginning to think that you're just a self-absorbed narcissist who is so obsessed with winning that you—"

She climbed off her bike and immediately

stopped talking as she scanned the scene. Her mouth fell agape. "What is this?"

Hawk stood off to the side with a hint of a smile on his face. "Go on, Alex. Don't let this stop you."

She slugged him in the arm. "You're such a jerk sometimes."

His eyes widened. "Do jerks plan surprise romantic picnics on Hawaiian mountainsides for their girlfriends?"

"Well, you definitely get points for creativity," she said as she moseyed over toward the table and then hovered over it, inspecting each item.

Hawk eased up behind her and gave her a hug. "Would you like to have a seat?"

She turned toward him and gave him a kiss. "I think I'd like that."

Hawk pulled out the chair for her and waited for her to sit down before nudging her seat closer to the table. He quickly joined her on the other side and signaled for one of the other men to begin.

Alex's eyes widened again as the sound of the ukulele began to play softly. The three men re-emerged from the nearby bushes and began singing several songs.

"I didn't even see them," Alex said. "Being on vacation has me off my game. I usually would've—"

"Noticed them?" Hawk asked. "You seem to have a lot on your mind at the moment. It's okay."

"It's just that—" she paused and turned, scanning the surrounding area before letting her gaze linger on the churning South Pacific. "It's been a long time since I haven't had to worry about anything and just be myself."

"Far too long," Hawk said. "For me too."

"I just want to stay here for a while."

Hawk took both of her hands in his and smiled. "We don't have anywhere to be right now." He took a deep breath before continuing. "But we do have some business to take care of."

Alex glanced over at the man still strumming the ukulele while the other two sang softly.

"Business?" she said as she withdrew her hands. "I thought you just said that—"

"Not that kind of business," he said as he slipped out of his chair and eased onto the ground next to her, kneeling.

He dug into his pocket and produced a box. He presented it open to her.

Alex stared down at the sparkling diamond and smiled before turning serious. "Where did you get this diamond?"

"Don't worry. It didn't support any terrorist cells. I checked."

She picked up the box and examined the ring more closely.

"Here," Hawk said, gently taking the box from her. "Let me give the ring a better setting."

He eased the ring onto her finger and smiled as her face lit up.

"Alex Duncan, will you marry me?"

She nodded, tears welling up in her eyes. He stood, and she leaped into his arms. The trio playing in the background broke into a more celebratory song. Hawk wasn't sure if the moment was about to be ruined by the three men, but that worry was quickly put to rest when Alex grabbed Hawk and started swinging him around.

"Maybe we could have a Bollywood-themed wedding," Hawk suggested.

Alex stopped, casting a sideways glance at him. "How about we do it right now?"

"Now? As it *right* now?"

She nodded. "I saw this little chapel on the beach. It'd be perfect."

"Okay," Hawk said. "What about your family?"

"The dysfunction that is both of our families—both biological and adopted—will excuse us for not wanting to deal with the stress of determining who to invite and who not to invite. I'm certain I'd give up if we went through all of that."

"Guess it sounds like we're getting married at a beachside chapel."

"Race you to the bottom," Alex said, jumping on her bike.

Hawk grabbed her arm. "Wait. Look over there."

He pointed toward a group of four men standing on a nearby cliff that soared more than four hundred feet above the beach.

"Are they doing what I think they're doing?" Alex asked.

Hawk nodded. "Just watch."

One of the men took off running and then leaped into the air, quickly pulling his ripcord and gently floating down to the beach. The others cheered and hollered with delight. Then the next man took off running.

Alex shook free of Hawk's grip and jumped on her bike, pedaling for thirty feet before he realized what was happening.

"See ya down there," she said.

Hawk turned and thanked the men, tipping them for their help as if they'd performed for the allotted hour. They sprang into action and started cleaning up, while Hawk jumped on his bike to chase Alex.

He'd seen the chapel, too, and entertained the idea of getting married there, but he didn't want to cheat Alex out of a big day. Based on how fast she was flying down the hill, she didn't mind.

Hawk's muscles burned as he tried to catch up

with her. The trail dipped and lurched, dropping down near dry gulches and climbing up toward scenic vistas near the water. While he tried desperately to catch up with her, he couldn't help but enjoy the sights and sounds of the wildlife. He'd realized that keeping his head down and looking only for targets had hampered his ability to just be. As the bike shimmied over a rocky area full of pebbles, Hawk couldn't wipe the grin off his face if he wanted to. Without anyone on his tail trying to kill him, the bike ride felt serene— and, in some ways, surreal.

Once Hawk finally reached the bottom, he still didn't see any sign of Alex.

She must've really flown on that bike.

Hawk looked to his left for cars and didn't see any. The road was practically barren save for a few locals puttering around in Volkswagen buses as they transported surfers and their boards down to the water's edge.

Where did she go?

Hawk zeroed in on the beachside chapel in the distance. There was only one car out front, but no bikes were secured by the bike rack. Alex was nowhere to be seen.

He pedaled over to the chapel and eased into the vacant reception area.

"Hello?" Hawk called. "Is anyone here?"

A few seconds later, a woman swam through the colorful beads serving as a makeshift door behind the desk.

"Aloha," she said. "May I help you?"

"Yes, I'm here looking for my girl—" Hawk stopped himself. "I'm looking for my fiancée. Do you know if anyone has happened by here in the past few minutes?"

"I believe she's on the back deck with my daughter getting a tour," the woman said. "She was rather excited to be here."

Hawk exhaled, relieved to hear the news. He followed the woman through the island-themed chapel and through the back doors. Alex was getting a full explanation of all the extras included in an Aloha Weddings package when she looked over at Hawk.

"You finally made it," she said. "What took you so long?"

Hawk put his right hand over his heart. "You scared me. I didn't see your bike out front and I—"

"I scared you?" she asked with a coy grin. "That's got to be a first."

"Things are different now," he said. Hawk asked the young woman giving the tour if they could have a moment alone. She agreed before retreating inside the chapel.

"Are you sure you want to do this right now?"

Hawk asked. "I mean you just said yes. You haven't even told anyone yet."

"Who else would I want to tell? Blunt?"

"I'm sure he already knew what we were going to do before we did."

Alex chuckled. "He's probably watching us right now."

Hawk's phone buzzed. He fished it out of his pocket to see who was calling.

"Well, speak of the devil," Hawk said. "It's Blunt calling now."

"Probably to congratulate us."

Hawk nodded in agreement before answering. "You just can't give us a moment of peace, can you?"

"You're not in the middle of your wedding ceremony, are you?" Blunt asked.

"Think we would get married without you here?"

Blunt ignored him. "Look, we've got a serious problem on our hands, and I need both of you as soon as possible."

"You sure it can't wait another few days?" Hawk asked. "We're just now starting to unwind and—"

"No, this can't wait. I've got a plane waiting for you that will take you straight back to Washington."

"What could be that important that I haven't even heard about it?" Hawk asked.

"There's a crisis in London, and Karif Fazil is at

the center of it."

"Crisis? What kind of crisis?"

"I can't really talk about this on an unsecure line, but long and short of it is that the Brits have lost scores of good agents, their bodies littered along the Thames."

"Who else has been exposed?"

"We don't know that yet, but the British need our help—more specifically, they need you and Alex. Sorry to ruin your vacation, but I wouldn't do it unless this was of utmost importance."

"Roger that. We're on our way." Hawk hung up and looked at Alex, her eyes pleading for him to ignore Blunt's request.

"Can't we just go back later?" Alex asked. "I'm sure they can hold up for a few more hours."

Hawk shook his head. "I hate this, but I don't want to rush this moment either. I want to savor it like I've been able to savor these past few days with you, days where work was the furthest thing from my mind."

She sighed. "Is this what it's going to be like?"

"What do you mean?"

"Us always running all over the world to stop some imminent threat?"

Hawk cocked his head and eyed her closely. "Don't act like that. I know you better than you think I do."

"Just answer the question."

"Of course it's going to be like this."

A smile leaked across her face. "Good. Because I wouldn't have it any other way."

CHAPTER 3

Iraq, undisclosed location

KARIF FAZIL CLASPED HIS HANDS behind his back and paced around the underground room. The vaulted ceilings above gave Jafar enough space to soar around when he grew tired of perching on Fazil's shoulder. Fazil glanced up occasionally to make sure Jafar was still overhead before putting his head back down and losing himself in his thoughts.

The past few months had been a whirlwind, full of mild successes tempered by abject failures. If one of his subordinates had such a track record, he would've helped him retire at the bottom of a shallow grave in the desert. But he wasn't about to subject himself to the same standard. He simply needed a new plan—one that struck at the heart of the enemy he loved to hate.

Yet something happened over the past month that changed everything for him. It only took one small piece of intel. It transformed his outlook on fighting against a foe with limitless resources and an ever-watchful eye in the sky. More than that, the news gave him hope that he could achieve what he wanted more than anything in his life: to avenge the death of his brother. With the pieces falling into place so rapidly, he could sense that opportunity drawing nearer as the odds increased in his favor with each passing day.

Jafar lit on a small ledge near the top of the rough-hewn ceiling. Jagged rocks looming above still served as a reminder that he was far from where he wanted to be, hidden from the drones combing the ground for one of his encampments. But such was the life Fazil chose when he pushed Al Hasib to the forefront of the global consciousness.

Jafar cooed and looked down. Knowing what his pet bird was after, Fazil dipped into his pocket and grabbed a handful of seeds. He held his palm flat and waited. Jafar lunged off his rock and swooped toward Fazil, before alighting on his shoulder. Fazil raised his hand closer so Jafar could snag the seeds with his beak.

"You know that pigeons are dirty birds, don't you?" said Kareem Khetran, one of Fazil's newly promoted assistants. Khetran had played a key role in helping secure a large cache of new intelligence, the kind that could swing the war on the west—the *jihad*—into Al Hasib's favor.

"You speak to me as if we're far more familiar than we are," Fazil said.

The brash young man didn't flinch. "Perhaps you need to surround yourself with more people who will speak the truth to you."

"The truth doesn't always get you what you want."

"And what is it that you think I want?" Khetran asked.

"I'm almost certain it's a bullet to the head if you continue acting as if you're the one in charge around here instead of me."

Khetran shrugged. "Maybe I just don't want you to fall ill at the hands of a bird that's the flying equivalent of a rat."

"That would be an honorable reason, but I don't believe it," Fazil said.

Khetran stroked his chin, tilting his head back in a pensive manner. "A wise man once told me that the truth doesn't always get you what you want. And the only conclusion I can draw from that is that it's better to lie on occasion to spare the listener the misery of the truth."

Fazil clapped slowly several times, each smack echoing around the room. "You're going to get exactly what I think you're looking for if you can't bridle your tongue."

Khetran put his hands in the air in a posture of surrender. "I can keep quiet. But please don't blame me when you get sick because of that bird."

Jafar took flight off Fazil's shoulder and soared overhead. After a few seconds, it dumped some excrement, which landed a few feet away from Khetran. He took a step back and looked up at the bird.

"You better be careful what you say around him," Fazil said. "He understands more than you might think."

Khetran scowled. "He's not ape or even a dog. He's a pigeon, one of the dumbest animals on the planet."

Another pile from Jafar landed closer to Khetran; this time a few drops splattered onto his shoe.

"Keep talking," Fazil said. "In this instance, perhaps the truth is more dangerous than you know."

Khetran sighed and shuffled backward, periodically glancing upward at Jafar.

"Now that you're done insulting my precious bird, you better pray to Allah that you give me the answer I'm looking for," Fazil said. "So, let's get down to business."

Khetran nodded and took a seat at the table in the center of the room across from Fazil.

"What is the latest on our recruitment efforts in London?" Fazil asked.

"At the moment, they are serviceable, though not as large as I hoped they would be."

"There are four locations I want to target," Fazil said. "Do you have at least a dozen men for each one?"

"We're working on it. Evana has told me that it's not as easy as you might think. London is full of Muslims, but mostly moderates."

Fazil sneered. "Those people aren't true Muslims. They simply want the peace that comes with following the Qaran, unaware that war comes with it. You can't pick and choose what you want. The Qaran isn't a buffet—it's a prescription."

He felt his face turn red, rage coursing through his veins. But Fazil's talk was just a cover. The real source of his anger was frustration and fear. Frustration that he hadn't been able to acquire all the assets necessary to complete a successful operation. Fear that he wouldn't be able to avenge his brother's death. The two emotions are what created Fazil's sleepless nights in recent weeks. If he didn't succeed, he didn't know what he'd do. He had put so much thought and planning into this mission that he was certain it would achieve his ultimate goal. But he wasn't about to let everything be undone by a lack of willing martyrs.

"Want me to put more pressure on Evana?" Khetran asked. "She might need to feel some heat to inspire her to take action."

Fazil held up his hand. "No, she has as much at stake in this operation as I do. We share a common goal with a common passion."

"Or so you think. Do you know what she does in London?"

Fazil nodded. "She has more access to recruits than we could ever dream of."

"So we just let her do her job and hope she finds the necessary participants?"

"Pack your bags," Fazil said. "We're going to London ahead of schedule."

CHAPTER 4

Washington, D.C.

BLUNT HOBBLED DOWN the steps into the bowels of the Pentagon. He kept his fedora pulled low over his brow, avoiding eye contact with any of the personnel scurrying through the hallways. While he'd made plenty of trips to the U.S. military's operation hubs on numerous occasions, he didn't want to attract any attention. The fewer people who knew of his presence here, the better.

He shuffled along and pondered the possibility that this could be his final visit to see General Van Fortner in his ivory tower paid for by the American people. Blunt wanted to be in a sailboat somewhere, something he'd tried and failed at once before. The president had managed to hunt Blunt down when he believed nobody could possibly find him. Since that time, Blunt had come to grips with the fact that it was impossible to escape the reach of the U.S.

government's covert operatives. It could take a long while to find someone, but they would eventually find their target. Blunt's dream of skimming across the calm waters of the Pacific Ocean and disappearing forever was truly unattainable. But that didn't stop him from yearning for such a thing. Quite the opposite happened, in fact. It only made Blunt desire for his twilight years all the more.

He just wanted to strike out on a new adventure. He longed to see the world from a different perspective, preferably one that wasn't in grainy satellite images through infrared lenses. All around him, the world was bursting with vivid colors and interesting personalities whose lives hadn't been beaten down by the laborious exercise of espionage.

Maybe Hawk and Alex can take over and run this thing without me. They don't really need me any more.

Blunt wasn't sure if he was lying to himself, but the thought was comforting. He could hand over the keys to the kingdom, in a manner of speaking, and let Hawk and Alex navigate Firestorm through all the political storms that Blunt had so adroitly handled through the years. Hawk would definitely rub them the wrong way at first, but he would mellow and so would the decision makers once they saw the kind of results that he got.

Blunt poked his head into the room where

Fortner was the lone occupant seated at the far end of the table.

"Long time, no see," Fortner said as he stood and walked over to shake Blunt's hand.

"If only that were the truth," Blunt said.

"It's been what? Three months?"

Blunt shrugged. "I think it's actually been four, but who's counting?"

"Please, have a seat," Fortner said, gesturing toward the head of the table.

"Me? Here?" Blunt asked, pointing at the seat. "Shouldn't this be your spot?"

"Your team is the invited guest of honor today. Without you and what they've been able to accomplish, we wouldn't be having this meeting."

Blunt sighed and shook his head. "So, it's my own damn fault then that I'm here and not out sailing somewhere?"

Fortner smiled. "I guess you could look at it that way—a victim of your own success in some respects. But without your successes, this world would be a different place right now, and you know it."

"I'm sure someone else would step up and fill the role," Blunt said as he settled into his seat.

"But nobody is as good as you. Stop with this humility shtick."

Blunt slung his briefcase onto the table and

pulled out several folders. "I'm not getting any younger. I just think it's time to pass the torch to some capable agents."

A military liaison rapped on the entrance of the door.

"Mr. Davenport is here," he announced.

"Thank you," Fortner said as he nodded at the man.

Davenport then strolled into the room, pausing only to shake Blunt's hand and make a brief introduction. Blunt stood.

"I've heard great things about you, Senator Blunt," Davenport said.

"All of them exaggerated, I'm sure," Blunt said as he eased back into his chair.

"Don't be so humble," Davenport said.

"People keep telling me that, but I'm just doing my job."

Davenport shook his head. "No, I know about what you've done to make this world more difficult for people like Karif Fazil. And that's not an easy task in this day and age. Tiptoeing through the political minefields is a chore for even the best statesman, let alone a master strategist from the field of espionage. You have a unique blend of both talents."

"I doubt they'll name any highways or schools after me. I'm just trying to protect our freedoms and keep these terrorist pukes living in fear themselves. The deeper we can push them into obscurity, the better."

Davenport took a seat next to Fortner. "I say the faster we can eradicate the bastards from the planet, the better. I don't want to share the same air as them."

Fortner smiled and looked at the British defense minister. "I like how you think."

"Unfortunately, it's not that easy," said a man from the hallway.

All three men at the table turned to look and see Hawk and Alex striding into the room. The pair of Firestorm agents sat next to Blunt.

"Mr. Hawk," Davenport said. "You're the man I've heard so much about. It's so nice to finally meet you."

Hawk reached over and shook Davenport's hand. "I wish we could be meeting under different circumstances, especially considering this crisis just resulted in us having to cut short our Hawaii vacation."

Davenport nodded. "Well, hopefully, we'll be able to get this resolved quickly and get you back out to that beautiful island before you know it."

"When Karif Fazil is involved, nothing gets resolved quickly," Hawk said.

"Well, let's get to it," Fortner said as he stood and walked across the room to close the door. "We have a big problem on our hands, and we need the team that knows Karif Fazil the best to help our friends."

"If the solution involves finally eliminating Fazil, that will help all of us," Alex said.

"Amen to that," Fortner said. "He's been a thorn in our side too. So, Mr. Davenport, the floor is yours."

Davenport passed out neat packets to all the meeting attendees, outlining all British intelligence knew about the agent body dump into the Thames. Blunt watched for Hawk and Alex's reaction, who were the only ones who didn't know what had been happening since they were happily out of touch with the real world in Hawaii. Since this discovery, Blunt's life had been consumed with calls, texts, and emails from the entire intelligence community worldwide, all abuzz with fear over the exposure of the British agents.

"If you'll look in your packets on page six, you'll see a brief explanation on how Al Hasib obtained this information and was able to do what they did," Davenport said. "The problem is we don't know how far this breach goes."

Blunt scanned his packet and grunted. "Black Wolf? I thought he was dead."

"We all did," Davenport said. "But apparently, he's not. His death was staged, and the Serbians were too embarrassed to share the truth with everyone else.

And thanks to your team, Senator, we know that the information Black Wolf was trying to pedal never made it into the hands of Al Hasib. However, what we don't know is what he actually has. Is it just British intelligence? Was that from a subsequent hack? Or did he have another file stashed away somewhere that puts all our agents at risk. Everyone I know in command is weighing the decision of pulling out their agents."

"You can't determine something like that lightly," Blunt said. "Our first priority needs to be our agents' safety, but the information we glean from them has thwarted many attacks. We would be having 9/11 events almost monthly if not for their work."

"This is all very interesting," Hawk said, looking up from the packet. "But why exactly are we here?"

* * *

DAVENPORT HAD ONE burning question, one that needed to be answered. He didn't want to start an American inquisition, especially where he was concerned. His goal for the meeting was simple. Get an answer on Fazil's tendencies in a situation like this and get back home.

Davenport shifted the papers in front of him, unable to avoid the Firestorm team's inquiries.

"Why are you here, Mr. Hawk?" Davenport began. "That's a good question. The bottom line is that you are the experts on Al Hasib and we need to know what you think his next move might be."

"In other words," Alex began, "do we think this is simply a one-off attack or an opening salvo in a war that's about to begin?"

"Precisely," Davenport said. "So, what are your initial thoughts on all of this?"

Alex shrugged. "It's hard to say at this point. Fazil always seems to have a plan that goes beyond what you initially see."

Hawk nodded in agreement. "You can never really tell with him, but I wouldn't relax at this point. The real question I have is why your country? Why the Brits? He's been attempting attacks on U.S. soil and U.S. interests abroad for a long time. This seems like a sudden change. That's what strikes me about this development more than anything."

Fortner turned toward Davenport. "Care to shed any light on this?"

Davenport shook his head resolutely. "I have no idea. This came out of the blue for me just as much for you as it did for me."

He sat back in his chair. He wasn't ready to tell the Americans the full truth—at least not yet.

CHAPTER 5

London, England

ALMOST A FULL WEEK had passed since Al Hasib littered the Thames with the bodies of dead agents. The stories appearing in every British tabloid varied wildly depending on the publication, providing entertaining reading. Theories consisted of everything from alien abductions to mafia hits. However, no one suspected terrorists, nor did any reporter uncover the fact that all of the dead were agents working for the British government.

Karif Fazil skimmed the articles and chuckled at some of the more outlandish ideas proffered by reporters. "I'm beginning to think the only news in the west is fake news. And to think that they used to sit upon a high horse and mock other countries for allowing the government to have a propaganda mouthpiece in the media?"

"It was a different era," one of the men seated

across from him said. "Journalism used to be about telling the truth. Now it's about selling a story, truth be damned."

Fazil narrowed his eyes and shoved the papers aside. "These people don't want to know the truth. They would rather live in their little naïve cocoons than deal with the impending reckoning that we will bring to their country for their actions against us."

Fazil's fiery comment was met with scattered applause from the other men in the room. He stood, shoving his chair back before climbing on top of the table. He seized the moment to inspire his troops.

"In the days ahead, we face a daunting task, one that will strike a blow at the illusion harbored by the British people. They believe they're safe, not to mention superior. They think that they can do whatever they want, whenever they want, to whoever they want. But we must teach them a lesson. We must show them that we will not be bullied. We will not be treated in such a manner. We will not allow the arrogance of the west to impose a heavy hand against us without paying a dear price."

Each statement Fazil made was affirmed by clapping and attendees nodding and shouting out comments like "yes" and "truth." It only encouraged Fazil to continue.

"Every one of you here knows what I'm talking

about," Fazil continued. "We've been pushed around, maligned by these countries. They speak of welcoming us with open arms, but the reality is they want to squash us. They think they hold the moral high ground. They call us terrorists when in reality we are freedom fighters. We will take back our dignity and this world. We will no longer be slaves to their whims, resigned to a second-class status. We will rule all of them."

The room erupted in applause.

"Now, let's get to work," Fazil said before jumping down off the table.

He watched as the men scattered across the room and began teaming up to work on various unfinished projects. Time was a precious commodity that was rapidly dwindling before Al Hasib accomplished its true mission in London.

Fazil looked at one of the men. "Without you, I'm not sure how much of this would've been possible. It's nice to have a man on the inside."

The man smiled back at him and nodded knowingly.

"There are others, you know?" a woman asked.

Fazil turned to see Evana Bahar standing a few feet away. "Others?"

"Yes, others on the inside. It's not just men who are joining in your fight."

Fazil nodded. "I've heard you are doing a serviceable job."

Bahar rolled her eyes. "You are no different than the people you hate. You have your own reasons for believing that you are superior, but you fall victim to the same type of arrogant thinking."

Fazil cocked his head. "Enlighten me."

"You think that because you are a man that you deserve to control everyone around you who's a woman, do you not?"

Fazil shrugged. "I follow the Qaran."

"The Qaran tells us to care for others and seek to humble ourselves, not seek a position of power and authority so we might suppress them."

"I also follow Mohammed as well."

She started to say something and then stopped.

"Do go on," Fazil said.

"I think I've said enough for now."

Fazil shook his head. "No, on the contrary, you haven't said enough. You like to think of yourself as someone who has moral high ground. You are better than me because—I'm not sure. But it is evident that you believe your way is superior. Talk about a hypocrite."

"My way is not bathed in arrogance, nor is it self-serving."

"Then why join Al Hasib's fight, cousin?"

Bahar stepped back and bit her lip. She stared off

in the distance pensively before returning her gaze to Fazil. "Your question contains the answer."

"And that is?"

"Family, Karif," she said. "We both lost people very dear to us that day. And justice must be served. But it must not extend beyond that."

"Then I would argue that what you seek is not true justice. You seek an even trade. But true justice takes back what was stolen and more."

"I don't see it that way."

"Give it time. You will come to see that these infidels will stop at nothing to poison the well. They will castigate us as the monsters when to find the true monster, all they need to do is look in the mirror. We are simply defending our way of life. And very soon we will show them that the consequences of treating us in this manner will be dire and costly."

She nodded. "Perhaps you are right, but that is a path I'm not yet ready to travel."

"You are too pure, cousin," Fazil said.

"Stop calling me that," she said. "You know that we are not related. Our parents were simply the best of friends, but we don't share blood."

Fazil grinned. "I'm keenly aware of that fact."

"We need to discuss the recruitment process," she said. "I'm not sure we have enough funds necessary to continue recruiting."

"Don't worry about the money. Allah will provide."

"Unless Allah has a bank account from which I can write these checks, we're not going to be able to gather many more recruits. And you can forget about any such operation in the future. No one will ever forget—or stop talking about—the time they were promised a large sum of money which was never delivered."

Fazil eyed her closely. "I know you, Evana. And I don't believe you were waving money in front of the recruits' faces. So how did you lure them into this dangerous task?"

"She promised us Heaven," one of the nearby men said as he dropped in on the conversation. He put his arms around Evana from behind and gave her a hug, one that seemed very familiar.

Fazil peered into Evana's eyes. "Heaven on earth?"

She rolled her eyes and pushed away the man who had slipped up behind her and chimed in without being invited. Fazil arched his eyebrows.

She wagged her index finger at Fazil. "I'm immune to your charm, Karif. Other women may fall for your rehearsed lines, but not this one. I am only here for the cause. I'm only here because I want justice, nothing less and nothing more."

Fazil shrugged. "You'll come around. Besides, we have much to discuss, particularly how this operation will be conducted."

"I am privy to your plans. There are other ways that you can accomplish the same end without sacrificing so much."

He narrowed his eyes. "Not if you want to inflict pain."

"So, this is about pain?" she asked.

Fazil nodded.

"His or yours?"

Fazil watched as Evana walked away. She had known him far too long, which was why she excelled at pushing his buttons. Yet he struggled to understand how come she couldn't see things his way. Evana's retaliation seemed more like responding to a punch with a mild push. If the Westerners believed that Fazil and his people only understood force, he would show them a force they would never forget.

He smiled as Evana sashayed through the cluster of men. She was definitely a new age woman, someone who lived with a foot squarely planted in the past and present, a paradox by anyone's definition. Yet not everyone looked so favorable upon her allegiances that seemed divided between the old and new. While some of the men on hand laughed and enjoyed her scandalous exit, others jeered her.

Fazil wasn't sure if he would ever ultimately accept such behavior on a regular basis as part of his faith, but he was certain of one thing: Eventually

Evana would come to see things from his perspective one way or another.

He whistled loudly, garnering the attention of everyone in the building.

"It's time to begin phase one," he announced.

CHAPTER 6

Kensington, London

LIAM DAVENPORT WATCHED the city blur past
as he drove along the M4 toward his home in
Kensington. He had plenty of time to think as traffic
along the motorway slowed, red lights blinking as the
drivers inched down the road. With a long sigh, he
pondered how his current status mirrored that of his
problem with Al Hasib. There were no shortcuts, just
a long hard route that required persistence if he
wanted to arrive safely and as quickly as possible. For
Davenport, the end of the journey couldn't arrive
soon enough, both figuratively and literally.

He loosened his tie and smiled at the thought of
seeing Evelyn, Ava, Millie, and Benjamin. But the reunion would be brief—and filled with questions. He
considered taking action before he left Washington,
but he wanted to do this in person. He called Evelyn,
but she didn't pick up.

Probably busy out with the children. I'm sure she'll call back soon.

Evelyn was a hardened military wife, but she'd lost most of her callousness since he'd taken a position with more predictability and zero combat. She expressed her gratitude often in both words and deeds for the change in his career path. But processing this sudden news alone while he was on another continent would be subjecting her to untold misery. She'd told him of how she rarely slept more than an hour or two while he was in combat missions in the Middle East all while trying to handle a preschooler, toddler, and a newborn. He never understood how she did it, but he could see the toll such a lifestyle had taken on her body every time he returned home. There were always a few more wrinkles, a few more strands of gray, a little less love.

Davenport's decision to move his family to the country and away from any potential attack by a vengeful Fazil was a wise one. But with it would come plenty of questions. Davenport had already fielded plenty from his advisors in both official and unofficial capacities. And he handled them well. However, Evelyn and the kids? He wasn't sure how he was going to navigate his way through their impending minefield of questions. Every answer would be followed up with another *why*. While he wasn't looking forward to satisfying their inquisition, he was confident he would and they would accept his decision.

I'll tell them it's like in Chronicles of Narnia. Maybe you'll find a wardrobe that will transport you to another world.

Ava might roll her eyes, or they might light up with anticipation. She was at a delicate age and one fraught with unpredictability. Half the time she acted as if she wanted to be a grown woman, while the rest of the time she behaved as an insufferable child, determined to be as petulant as possible.

Benjamin and Millie would get excited about such a suggestion. The idea of riding horses around in a forest full of talking beavers and mythical creatures was one both would find appealing—as long as they could get back home.

Davenport smiled at the thought. Given his current circumstances, his family was about the only thing that could wipe the worried look off his face. The rest of his life was a pressure cooker, just waiting to explode.

When traffic crawled to a stop, he activated the hands-free calling feature on his cell phone and dialed the office. Melissa answered.

"I'm on my way back to my house," Davenport said. "What is the word on the transport for Evelyn and the children?"

"There haven't been any problems. I have the

driver scheduled to arrive in just over an hour. Is that sufficient time for you to speak with them and to let them gather their belongings? Or do we need to extend the time?"

"That should suffice," he said. "Thank you for setting that up for me."

"You're welcome. Glad you made it back safely. Any idea when you're planning on coming into the office? Because I need your authorization on quite a few requests."

"Just leave them on my desk. I'll probably come in later this evening, especially since I'll have no reason to be at home."

"Very well then. I'll see you at the office in the morning."

Davenport hung up and continued to navigate through traffic. His mind drifted back toward the looming crisis. Without any idea of how long it would last, the thought of his family being away from him for an extended period of time was disconcerting. One of the perks of becoming the Minister of Defense was to be close to his family, but now they needed to go far away because of it. Or to be more exact, because of a decision he made. Not that he would change anything necessarily.

Maybe I should've told the Americans.

It was too late now, water under the proverbial

dam. If the opportunity arose to tell them at the right time, he would. But there was no opportunity, and this wasn't the time. Davenport wondered if there ever would be either.

When Davenport arrived home, he parked his car along the curb and hustled up to the front steps. Evelyn always made a big deal out of his homecoming after being gone. The children would draw him pictures, she would make one of his favorite meals, and the house would be spotless.

Davenport found it odd that the lights were out, though Evelyn had yet to call him back. She was probably playing chauffeur with Ava, Benjamin, and Millie. Davenport hadn't checked his schedule to see what was on it. He wasn't even sure what day it was.

When he went to open the door, it was locked. He pulled out his key and twisted it in the lock, opening the door. He pushed his way inside and called out to his family.

"Evelyn? Millie? Benjamin? Ava? Is anyone home?"

He half expected Ava to wander out of the darkness, staring at a device with one earbud in. But if anyone was home, they weren't making a sound.

"Evelyn?"

Still nothing.

Davenport headed toward the kitchen but nearly

slipped on a soccer ball. He regained his balance before flipping on the nearest light switch. Peering into the adjacent playroom, he noticed pictures strewn about. The house was a disaster.

This isn't like Evelyn.

He pulled out his cell phone and dialed her number again. Tapping nervously on the doorjamb, he waited for her to pick up and explain everything.

Four rings, five rings. Nothing. Voicemail.

You've reached Evelyn. Leave a message, and I'll get back to you as soon as I can.

Davenport didn't need to say anything. She always called him back within seconds once she saw his number, but her lack of response prompted him to record a short note.

"Hey, love. It's me. I'm getting a little worried since I haven't heard from you yet. I made it back safely and am at the house now. I'm sure you're out running around with the children. Please do call me whenever you get a spare second. I can't wait to see you."

He hung up and stared at his phone long enough to see the minute on the clock move one digit. Without wanting to wait for her to explain, he flipped over to their joint family calendar to see what was on the day's docket. His mouth fell agape when he came to the date.

The date was empty.

According to Evelyn, there wasn't anything going on that constituted being put on the calendar. He thought it might have been a mistake, so he scrambled back to a week ago. Nothing on that date either. The one day each week when nothing happened was Monday—and today was indeed Monday.

So, where are Evelyn and the children?

Davenport opened an app on his phone that allowed him to see the location of his wife's cellular device.

She never goes anywhere without that thing.

He waited anxiously as the app searched for her location. A map materialized on the screen and showed the location.

Her phone is in the house?

He set down his briefcase and eased into his study where he had a gun hidden. Then he pinged her phone, setting off a loud beeping noise, the kind he used to find it for her when she'd misplaced it. The noise came from upstairs.

With both hands on his gun, he crept up the stairs. He'd lived in the house long enough to know which steps to avoid if he wanted to make a silent ascent. Sweat beaded on his forehead as he reached the landing. He held his breath and listened for anything other than the beeping sound.

A few seconds went by and nothing.

Then a thump.

He spun in the direction of the noise only to find Mr. Muggles, who had obviously jumped off some piece of furniture. Mr. Muggles sauntered over to Davenport and rubbed against his leg.

Davenport stole into the bedroom where the phone was and turned off the alert sound. All that was left was the guttural purring coming from Mr. Muggles and the limb of a tree he should've trimmed months ago tapping the side of the house to the rhythm of the wind.

He was more than worried—he was panicked.

Davenport dialed his assistant. "I need to speak to someone at operations," he said as soon as she answered.

"What's wrong?"

"It's Evelyn and the kids," he said. "They're missing."

CHAPTER 7

Washington, D.C.

HAWK INSPECTED THE BOTTLE of scotch in his hands. He wasn't certain Blunt would like it, but he would appreciate the gesture. Blunt had given Hawk a hard enough time about preferring bourbon that the gift would make Blunt consider the fact that he'd won Hawk over. Hawk still hated the stuff, but he was starting to understand that importance of statesmanship.

Alex rang the doorbell and glanced at Hawk's bottle before looking up at his face. "Are you really gonna drink that stuff?"

He shrugged. "If he offers it to me."

"It's too expensive. He'll probably shelve it and save it for a rainy day."

"Wanna make a bet on that?"

She eyed him closely. "What are the terms?"

Hawk thought as he heard plodding footsteps

near the door. "Loser has to buy dinner at the winner's restaurant of choice."

"We're engaged," she said. "That's a lame consequence."

"Nothing's lame about winning," he said as he winked at her.

The door swung open, and Blunt greeted them with open arms.

"Come in, come in," he said before glancing down at the bottle in Hawk's hands.

Blunt grabbed the bottle and removed his glasses briefly to inspect the label up close.

"I was hoping you'd heard of this scotch," Hawk said. "It was on the more expensive end."

Blunt nodded. "So I see. And this is why I've never been tempted to buy it. I'm always leery about committing to such a big investment with my scotch when I haven't tried it."

"Well, I—*we* hope you like it."

Blunt gestured toward the living room. "I'll take your coats, and you can come in and have a seat."

Hawk and Alex obliged, piling their jackets on top of Blunt's arm. He disappeared for a few seconds into a nearby office before returning. Hawk and Alex hadn't moved.

"Well, don't just stand there," Blunt said. "Let's move in here so we can sit down and be comfortable while we talk. Dinner will be ready in half an hour or so."

They all eased into the living room and sat down. Blunt popped back up to his feet almost as soon as he'd taken a seat.

"I'm sorry," he said. "Where are my manners?" He snagged the bottle of scotch off the table. "Would either of you like a glass?"

Hawk smiled slyly at Alex. "I'll take a glass, neat."

"Alex?" Blunt asked.

"I prefer drinks that are more fruity in nature."

"Would you like a margarita? It'll only take me a minute to make one."

She shook her head. "I shouldn't be rewarded with a drink after losing."

Blunt scowled. "What do you mean by that?"

She waved him off. "Never mind. It'd take too long to explain, and we have other things that are more important to discuss."

"That we do," Blunt said as he sauntered over to the wet bar in the corner of the room.

He poured two glasses and then rejoined them.

Blunt smiled after taking a sip. "I must say that I'm not entirely surprised. I could sense some good chemistry between you from the moment we started working together—and I'm not just talking about how you worked with one another on missions."

Hawk raised his glass. "I guess you deserve a toast as the unexpected matchmaker."

Blunt chuckled. "I don't know of an agency around that would celebrate such a thing. Two operatives getting married would be forbidden and seen as a move that would make both more vulnerable. Remaining unattached is the best way to operate in the world of espionage."

"Is that why you never remarried?" Alex asked.

"Who told you I was ever hitched?" Blunt asked with a furrowed brow.

"I read your file. You tried to keep it a secret, but someone found out about it."

"That was a long time ago, but I've moved on. In fact, I'm thinking about moving on permanently, which is why I invited the two of you over here tonight."

"How permanent are we talking about?" Hawk asked.

Blunt winked. "Not that permanent. And I'm not even considering faking my death again to do it. Getting to witness your own funeral is something I don't care to experience again."

"You're going to quit Firestorm?" Hawk asked.

"That's the idea, though that depends on a few things," Blunt said.

"Such as?" Alex asked.

Blunt took a long pull on his drink before setting the glass down on the coffee table in the center of the sitting area.

"For starters, I hate leaving a job undone," Blunt said.

"I recall you telling me on more than one occasion that the job of fighting terrorism is never finished," Hawk said. "Has something changed?"

Blunt flashed a smile. "No, it hasn't. But that's the problem. Karif Fazil is still running Al Hasib—and I made a promise to that senate committee a few years ago that we would take out Fazil and cripple Al Hasib. And for all the attacks we've staved off recently, I feel like we've failed in a major way. Al Hasib seems to be growing stronger, and Fazil is still very much alive."

"Let's put that aside for a moment," Hawk said. "Now, I've known you for a long time. And I know that you have to stay busy. How on earth would you fill up your time? You're not seriously thinking of retiring, are you?"

"I'll keep myself busy. Don't you worry. And what I'm considering doing would be called retirement in anyone's book."

"Which is what?" Alex asked as she shifted to the front of her seat.

"I want to get a nice boat and sail around the world."

"By yourself?" she asked.

"I have a few military buddies that might be persuaded to join me, but I'm not planning on having a party yacht."

Hawk grunted.

"What?" Blunt asked. "You're starting to sound like me."

"How? Communicating disapproval through guttural sounds? I kind of like this approach."

Blunt smiled. "See, you're more prepared than you know to take over my role with the team."

"But I was serious about my disapproval," Hawk said.

"You have reservations about this?" Blunt asked.

"For starters, didn't you try already when you were dead?"

"People were actually looking for me, people with means and motive," Blunt said. "This time, I think everyone will be happy to just let me float away into oblivion."

"I'm not sure Karif Fazil will be so forgiving."

Blunt shook his head. "He's got bigger fish to fry."

"Perhaps, but you also have made enemies all across the globe. Who's to say you don't go into port somewhere and someone sees you? You know that ports are a hotbed for espionage activity. And you have a face that's been plastered all over the news."

"But not necessarily in conjunction with our activities," Blunt said, continuing to defend his position. "Hardly anyone knows about my affiliation to Firestorm."

"All it takes is one."

"I think I've proven I can handle myself."

Hawk sighed. "Well, if there's anything else I've learned from working with you over the years, it's that you are stubborn and I won't be able to talk you out of this, no matter how well I appeal to reason."

"Damn right, you won't," Blunt said. He leaned forward and grabbed a cigar box off the table. He jammed a stogie into his mouth and chewed on it as the conversation continued.

"So, what will this look like moving forward?" Alex asked.

Blunt shrugged. "Not sure yet. We still have the tiny little detail of weakening Al Hasib and exterminating Karif Fazil."

"Hypothetically speaking, let's say we get that done in the next month or so," Hawk said. "I'm sure you've already got a plan."

Blunt held up his index finger as his cell phone started ringing. "Hold that thought." He exited the room to answer the call.

Hawk looked at Alex. "What do you think?"

She shook her head. "I can't imagine doing this without him. He's been such a great mentor and now a friend."

"I feel the same way, but this isn't completely surprising to me. We had to do this once before when he was supposedly dead. We can do it again."

"I guess you're right."

Hawk's hand shot up in the air, gesturing for Alex to be quiet. He thought he heard something and crept toward the entryway where Blunt's office was located.

"What are you doing?" Alex whispered.

Hawk waved her off and craned his neck to listen in.

"What is it?" she whispered again.

He looked back toward her. "This doesn't sound good."

Hawk heard Blunt close the conversation and shuffled toward the door. After tiptoeing back across the room, Hawk sat down and awaited Blunt's return.

"What is it?" Hawk asked as soon as Blunt reappeared.

"I hate to cut this short, especially with those marinated steaks I have on the grill outside and the fact that we've barely discussed anything about your engagement, let alone how Hawk proposed."

"It was pretty epic," Alex said.

"It looked that way," Blunt said. "I only wish the satellite feed had sound to accompany it."

Alex withdrew. "You were watching us?"

"I need to contact you in an emergency, but we can discuss that later. We have another emergency that's cutting our dinner short."

"What's happening?" Hawk asked.

"That was one of Davenport's aides. There's been a development. The British minister of defense has requested that we join him in London immediately."

"Why? What for?" Alex asked.

"His entire family has been kidnapped by Al Hasib."

Hawk's eyes widened. "That sounds personal to me. Fazil wouldn't take a risk on something like that abroad if he didn't have a serious motive."

"What was Davenport not telling us?" Alex asked.

"I don't know," Blunt said, "but his aide told me there was more to the story. Apparently, Davenport wants to tell us everything in person. They've chartered a plane for us that's being fueled up as we speak. Wheels up in an hour. You've got just enough time to swing by your place and pack before meeting me there."

Hawk and Alex stood and didn't linger, striding straight toward the door.

"See you in an hour," Alex said.

* * *

BLUNT CLIMBED THE STEPS to the second floor where his bedroom was. He couldn't tell if the creaking was coming from his knees or the stairs. Either way, it reminded him that he needed to move his bedroom to the ground level.

He yanked a suitcase down from the top of his closet and snatched a few clothes off the hangars to pack. His phone rang, arresting his attention.

What now?

He didn't recognize the number, but he answered the call.

"Senator Blunt?" asked a woman on the other end.

"Speaking."

"This is Camille Youngblood from *The Washington Post*. I was wondering if I could have a moment of your time."

"I would be more than happy to chat with you, but now isn't a good time," Blunt said matter-of-factly.

"I'm afraid this can't really wait," she said.

"It's gonna have to. You have no idea what's going on right now."

"Honestly, I don't care. I have a job to do, and I strongly suggest you speak with me now or else I'll move forward writing this story without your comment."

"What kind of story are you writing?"

"I know about Firestorm, Senator. And soon, the rest of the world will, too."

CHAPTER 8

London, England

KARIF FAZIL CIRCLED a seated Evelyn Daven-port, gently caressing her cheek with the back of his hand as he strolled past. She winced and tried to withdraw from his touch but was hampered by the ropes binding her to the chair. While Fazil preferred to inflict torture of a more physical nature, the mind games he was playing with his prisoner he found to be entertaining.

Fazil stopped and knelt in front of her. "There's no reason for you to be afraid. Your children are unharmed, and I have yet to hurt you."

"My husband will find me, and he's going to have you killed."

Fazil threw his head back and laughed. "I love your spirit, Evelyn. You're so confident, even while strapped down and completely helpless." He stood and continued pacing. "However, your faith in your husband is not grounded in reality. He's just a figure-head, although a very important one."

"What has my husband ever done to you?" she asked, still struggling with the bindings.

He walked up behind her and cinched the ropes tighter.

Fazil ran his index finger along the contours of Evelyn's body. He smiled with delight as she squirmed away from him in an effort to protect herself. After a minute of such silent persecution, he stopped and knelt back down in front of her.

"What has your husband ever done to me?" Fazil asked with a snarl. "That is a question I could answer for you rather easily, but I prefer you see the shallow grave where they threw my little brother's body for yourself."

He held up his cell phone, displaying a picture of a dead young boy along with a handful of others piled haplessly in a hole. She glanced at the photo and then diverted her eyes.

"Look at it," Fazil roared. "Don't turn away. This is what your husband did. He's the one who ordered the airstrike that destroyed my family. He's the one who thought that the collateral damage that went along with killing a terrorist was acceptable."

Fazil stood.

"Well, it's not acceptable," he said, stomping his

foot. "My little brother was a child with his whole life ahead of him, but it was snuffed out by a monstrous act, one dictated by your husband."

Evelyn narrowed her eyes. "And what about the lives of all the innocent people your father destroyed?"

Fazil's eyes widened.

"Yes, I know whose son you are," she said. "You don't get to claim any moral high ground in a fight your father started."

Fazil clenched his fists and took a deep breath. He wanted to beat the woman who dared to mock him. If he didn't have other plans for her, her comments were enough to warrant a fatal attack. No infidel had ever spoken to him in such a manner and lived, though she wouldn't either. Her end would come in a far less delicate way at a pre-appointed time. Knowing she would be wiped from the face of the earth very soon subdued his rage, yet holding his temper was still a challenge.

"The fight was brought to our soil," he said. "We had no choice."

"You always have a choice, yet you chose poorly."

"You're quite mouthy for a woman whose life is in my hands."

She glared at him. "If you wanted me dead, you would've already killed me by now."

Fazil smirked. "You seem to have forgotten that I also have your children in another room down the hall."

She growled. "If you dare lay a hand on any of them—"

"You'll what?" Fazil said before breaking into a laugh. "Woman, you have no idea what fate is about to befall you."

He eased closer to her and grabbed her jaw, jerking it upward toward him.

"Don't make threats you're incapable of fulfilling."

He released her, shoving her head backward. "You know nothing of the pain of losing someone unjustly. Imagine how you would feel if one of your daughters was—how should I put this—mistreated?"

"No," Evelyn cried, her bravado fading. "Do anything you want to me, but leave my daughters out of this."

"Since you believe in choice so much, I think I'll let you choose who we should start with—the older one or the younger one."

"You sick bastard," Evelyn screamed, struggling with her bindings. "I hope you burn in hell."

Fazil turned his back to her and shook his head. "And just when I thought we were coming to an understanding, Evelyn."

Evana emerged from the shadows and delivered

two vicious blows to Evelyn's face, the second one sending her sprawling backward in her chair. Her head thumped hard against the concrete floor, knocking her out.

Evana stood over her captive before glaring back at Fazil.

"Why does it take a woman to do a man's job these days?" she asked.

Fazil scowled. "Don't push me."

"I'll do whatever I want," Evana said. "You need me, and without my help on this operation, you'd be destined for another failure like all the others—San Francisco, New York, Washington. If we don't succeed this time, it won't be on my account. It'll be on yours . . . again."

"You're venturing into dangerous territory," Fazil said. "Be careful. Everyone is expendable."

"Even you," Evana snarled. "Don't lose your nerve to do what needs to be done. If you do, all these sacrifices will be in vain."

Fazil ignored Evana as she walked out of the room. He had special plans for her when everything was finished. Nobody would be permitted to speak to him in that way without severe consequences.

CHAPTER 9

Ministry of Defense Whitehall
London, England

LIAM DAVENPORT SWALLOWED HARD before thrusting open the doors to the conference room and striding toward his seat at the head of the table. The emergency gathering resulted in a collection of important dignitaries and agency heads. The leader of every branch of the military along with MI5 and MI6 directors also were there as were several members of parliament along with other deputies. Glancing toward the back wall, he noticed the three Americans he had begged to come.

After a deep breath, he took a seat and began the meeting. "I would like to thank you all for coming today on such a short notice," Davenport said. "I know that you're all busy dealing with this crisis in one way or another. But I feel like this time together will help bring clarity on what's at stake and how we can resolve this situation expediently."

He opened a folder and sifted through some papers. Clasping his hands together and resting them on the table in front of him, he continued. "While this attack seemed to come out of nowhere, I believe I know why it has been so swift and vicious. Several years ago, I authorized a drone strike that killed Fahad Osmani at a wedding. For three years, we had hunted him and finally got confirmation that he would be in a setting where we could finally eliminate him. The problem was the setting—a family wedding."

Several moans were heard around the table.

"Now, I know what you're thinking. *How could he be so reckless?* But the truth was we needed a win. Removing someone as important at Osmani meant that we could gain some of the ground we had lost in the war on terror. His cells were multiplying quickly due to his charismatic personality. We couldn't miss our opportunity to strike. Then when we found out that more than a dozen of Osmani's top lieutenants would be there, I knew this could be more than just a win. It could be a total decimation of one of the most dangerous terrorist organizations on the planet. At that point, I quit caring about collateral damage. As fate would have it, Karif Fazil is the bastard son of Fahad Osmani."

He took a sip of water and then continued. "In

hindsight, the situation could've been handled differently. But there's still time to manage this without it getting chaotic. Some part of me is worried about offending a community of people that is growing large and powerful right here in our own city. So I want to be cautious moving forward."

Brady Hawk raised his hand from the back of the room. Davenport wasn't finished, but he welcomed the interruption, giving him an opportunity lose the shade of red that blanketed his face.

Davenport nodded toward Hawk, resulting in every head in the room to turn on a swivel and look back toward him.

"This is Mr. Hawk who has been entangled many times with Karif Fazil and knows him better than anyone," Davenport said. "I invited him here to share his thoughts with us. Do you have a question, Mr. Hawk?"

Hawk shook his head. "I want to tell you that proceeding with caution will get you killed when it comes to confronting Fazil. He is ruthless and relentless. If you plan on taking him down, you need to use maximum force and worry about the collateral damage later."

"That's what got us into this mess," the MI6 director said. "We mustn't repeat the same mistake twice."

"No," Hawk said. "Using maximum force isn't what got you into this predicament. A determined zealot did. He wants to bring down his wrath upon you; make no mistake about it."

"No one here wants to engage in a jihadist war waged on the streets of London, but that's exactly what you're suggesting," Davenport said.

Hawk eased out of his chair and stood. "This is no longer about jihad or any specific cause other than Karif Fazil exacting revenge on Davenport and the British military for their actions in the desert that day. Fazil has done a fantastic job of cloaking every bomb, every terrorist act, every death as a response to the west, but it's never been about that for him. It's always been about the fact that he lost his brother and most of his family in an attack at a wedding full of innocent people. But instead of wiping out Fahad Osmani's organization, the action has sown more seeds of terror than anyone ever conceived."

Davenport gave Hawk a slight head nod. "Thank you for your input, Mr. Hawk. I knew you would share an unbridled opinion devoid of any political trappings that most of us around this table must deal with."

Davenport rubbed his temples with his fingertips.

"So, what do we need to do next?" one of the generals asked. "Is this a brainstorming session or the moment where we get our marching orders?"

Davenport shrugged. "Moving forward is complicated, as you might have guessed since Fazil has kidnapped my entire family. I have offered to resign, but that idea has been rejected by many of the leaders around this table. So, I bring it to you as a group. What should be our next move? I'm afraid my focus is singular at the moment, and I need all the help I can get to see the big picture. My myopic view right now isn't going to help us get what we're really after. All I want is to see my wife and children again."

"What are his demands?" the MI5 director asked.

"An even trade," Davenport said. "Me for my family."

"Absolutely not," said Admiral Sir Hugh Riley, the first sea lord of the Royal Navy. "The moment you start meeting their demands is the moment everything goes awry. Each one of us would then be susceptible to having our families nabbed in order to force our hands. The ministry of defense would never be able to rebuild such lost trust with our people once that information became public."

"But if I don't turn myself over to them, they will kill my entire family," Davenport said as he fought back tears.

"How do you expect that to play out exactly?" asked Alex from the back of the room. "Do you think he's just going to let them go?"

Davenport nodded. "He wants me, not my family."

"No," Hawk said. "He wants to make you suffer. This whole situation is personal to Fazil. You killed his family. He's probably relishing the opportunity to kill yours, only he wants to make you watch."

"He'd never get anything he wanted after that," Davenport said.

"That *is* what he wants," Hawk said. "You need to understand that if you're going to understand anything about Karif Fazil. He's not some idealistic crusader, pitting his faith against the west. He's a man hell-bent on getting revenge. And if you give yourself over to him, he's going to get that in a way that brings him the most unimaginable pleasure."

"Then what do you recommend doing? A rescue team? We don't even know where they are."

Hawk shrugged. "I'm not sure yet. But I do know that he probably believes you won't comply. You know, the whole 'we don't negotiate with terrorists' mantra. He knows you won't have the power to authorize anything on your own, so he's likely moving forward in the full expectation that you won't willingly give yourself over to him, which would be the worst thing that could happen in this situation."

"If it saves my family, it would be worth it."

"But it's not going to save your family," Hawk said. "Stop thinking that way. Now, when is this exchange supposed to take place?"

Davenport rubbed his forehead and slumped over in his chair. He took his time to respond. "They said they would text me with the exact time and location, but it's scheduled for tomorrow. I was never supposed to tell anyone."

"He's no fool," Hawk said. "He knows you wouldn't keep this ordeal entirely private, but he's not going to make himself too vulnerable. Wherever he decides to meet, he's going to have an exit strategy. We just have to figure out what that might be and cut him off before he gets away."

"With my family in the way? I'm not sure that's the best idea."

"At this point, do you have a better idea? If we do nothing, they're already as good as dead."

Davenport dismissed the meeting but requested that a few key tactical thinkers remain behind to discuss the implementation of an extraction plan. When the room was all but clear of a handful of people, he couldn't hold his emotions in any longer.

"He's going to kill them all, isn't he?" Davenport asked as tears streamed down his face. "That bastard is going to make me watch all of them die."

Hawk, who'd stayed behind, didn't affirm

Davenport's fears. "I've been in some tight spots going up against Fazil. We'll all do our best to prevent anything like that from happening, but you have to trust us. Can you do that?"

With quivering lips, Davenport nodded. But he didn't mean it.

Davenport wasn't sure he could trust anyone but himself with his family's life on the line.

CHAPTER 10

London, England

BLUNT WAVED THE KEY CARD over the security panel and waited for the door to click open. Once the light turned green, he turned the handle and slipped his way inside. He had turned down a call during Davenport's meeting while letting the Firestorm team do all the talking. As crazy as it sounded, Blunt had more pressing matters to attend to.

He listened to the voicemail and then dialed the callback number for *The Washington Post* reporter Camille Youngblood.

"Miss Youngblood, this is J.D. Blunt."

"Senator," she said. "I wasn't sure if you were going to call me back."

"Sorry, I'm just out here trying to save the world. What can I help you with? Your message sounded somewhat urgent."

She sighed. "It is. I have to tell you that I can't sit

on this story much longer. My editor has requested that I do my due diligence in at least asking you a few questions. How you answer them will go a long way in how you and your agency are portrayed in the story."

"What agency?" Blunt asked.

"Oh, don't be daft. You're not going to appreciate having all this evidence made public next to you appearing like some political stooge lying through your teeth."

"Writing such a story would be reckless," Blunt said.

"Why's that? The American people deserve to know how their tax dollars are being spent."

Blunt chuckled. "Trust me. The American people don't want to know where every dime is going. Nor can our government function with the citizens up in arms and trying to control how all their taxes are spent."

"No, that's exactly what the American people need to know. A government that goes unchecked runs amok."

"And you think telling America about the alleged existence of some black ops agency is going to help how? Most people generally accept the idea that these groups are real. And most people see them as beneficial, protecting our freedoms and halting potential threats against this country."

"But when they are used to overthrow democrat-ically elected leaders, including their own president," she said, letting her words hang.

"If you're insinuating what I think you are, you're way off base. Such accusations will find you and your paper in a heap of trouble."

"I'm just doing my job."

"I guess you are if your job is endangering the lives of American citizens through reckless reporting. In that case, you ought to win a Pulitzer."

"Just know that I'm recording this conversation."

"I don't care if you record this or not. Any tape of this conversation will only forever mark you as the one responsible the next time there's a terrorist attack on American soil or on American interests abroad. The real member of the media—the ones who dare to do their job right—will search for a place to lay the blame. And I'll have to remind them that an alleged black ops program that prevented dozens of such in-cidents in the past was attacked by one of their own. I wonder how quickly you'd last out there before the savages tore you apart and ended your career. But, hey, if it's worth that for a flashy headline for you for a few fleeting months, be my guest. Write whatever you want."

"Don't you dare threaten me," Youngblood said.

"I'm not threatening you. I'm just letting you know what will happen. I'm very good at reading people and understanding the country's mood. I never would've lasted long in office if I wasn't."

"Greasing the palms of every donor who drops some coin into your coffers is what keeps politicians in power."

Blunt chuckled. "You're far more ignorant than you think if that's what you believe it takes to remain in power. You actually have to do something for the people, too. And to do something for them that they will appreciate, you have to understand them. But don't worry. I understand journalists, too. I know they have an agenda, which is very simple: get the big story before someone else does. Become a hero among your peers. Maybe even win a few awards for your muckraking."

"You can deride my profession all you want, but the world needs to know about what you and your agency are doing."

"And why exactly is that?"

"Because you're doing some illegal shit, that's why."

"No, we keep Americans just like you safe every day." Blunt paused from his defense and attempted to appeal to reason in another way. "Let me ask you a question," he said. "Do you ever go watch the Nationals play?"

"Yeah. Who doesn't in Washington?"

"I know. I know. Nationals Park is the trendy place to go. So, imagine you're at the stadium and the entire structure collapses and kills thousands of innocent people who just wanted to watch a baseball game."

"What's your point, Senator?"

"That almost happened—but it didn't. Now I can't speak to what exactly happened, but perhaps this mythical agency you're talking about was the one that stopped this attack."

"Can you verify this attack happened?"

"I'm not verifying that the purported black ops team even exists. What makes you think I'm going to go on record and say anything about that potential attack that was avoided?"

"The end doesn't justify the means, Senator. There needs to be oversight with any group operating above the law."

"If this group exists, it's damn good at policing itself."

"That sounds like a recipe for disaster. All it would take is one rogue agent who has access to weapons and power. He could do unthinkable things."

"Disaster is what happens when someone else uses war and violent conflicts for political or financial gain. This group you're talking about probably handles such threats against this country, preventing the opportunity for corruption among its statesmen while making the threat itself vanish." Blunt took a deep breath and exhaled slowly before continuing. "I'm begging you not to write this because of the damage it will cause the countless lives in this country."

"Time's up, Senator." Youngblood hung up the phone.

Blunt cursed loudly and often as he paced around his hotel room. The public disclosure of Firestorm would be the end of the program, a fact he was all too aware of. After a minute of contemplating a way to shut down the article, he poured himself a glass of scotch. If he tried to use his leverage at the newspaper to force the article to be quashed, the action would only prove Youngblood's sources were right, whoever they were. She'd feel vindicated and parade a victory lap in front of him on the front page of not just *The Washington Post*, but also on the cover of every newspaper in the country.

A knock interrupted his contemplative mood.

He peeped through the hole before opening the door.

"Helluva meeting," Blunt said as he waved Hawk and Alex inside.

Hawk nodded. "This city doesn't know it's sitting on powder keg."

"It's probably better if they didn't," Blunt said before downing more of his scotch.

"Are you okay?" Alex asked.

"Okay with what?" Blunt asked gruffly.

"It sounded like you were upset about something in here," she said.

He waved dismissively. "It's not anything for you to be worried about."

"Spill it," she said as she sat down on the couch. "We're all family here."

Blunt sighed and settled into a chair in the sitting area of his hotel suite. He set his glass down on the coffee table then rubbed his face with both hands before groaning.

"That good, huh?" she asked.

"I've got a big problem, and her name is Camille Youngblood," Blunt said.

"That reporter at *The Washington Post?*"

Blunt nodded and kept his gaze fixed on the floor. "Bingo. Also known as a persistent pain in my ass."

"What's going on this time?" Alex asked.

"Apparently, someone leaked some information to her proving the existence of Firestorm."

He waited a moment before looking up. Both Hawk and Alex were staring at him slack-jawed.

"Nobody in that damn town can keep a secret."

"Well, it could only be a handful of people,"

Hawk said. "I'm sure we could figure out who it was and corner them."

"The damage will be done by then."

Hawk paced around the room, stopping briefly to look down onto the busy London street below.

"I've got an idea," he said.

"I hope it involves solving our problem with Miss Youngblood," Blunt said.

"Actually, I think this is a two-for-one deal," Hawk said.

"What other problem are you going to solve today, Hawk?" Alex asked with a wink.

"We've got one in London and one in Washington. And I think there's a way we can use Miss Youngblood to solve both of them for us."

"And how the hell do you intend to do that?" Blunt asked.

Hawk grinned. "We give her a better story."

"A better story than the one she's got. I can't think of anything better than—"

"Don't finish that sentence," Hawk said. "You know you've got plenty of things that would trump a lame story about a secret black ops group that everyone and their brother is already confident exists."

"Fair enough, but how is that going to help us here? You know Davenport doesn't want this leaking to the press."

"Of course he doesn't," Alex said. "He has too much to lose over this ordeal." She looked at Hawk. "But you're gonna do it anyway, aren't you?"

Hawk scooted up to the edge of his seat and leaned forward. "Look, we know that Davenport doesn't want this happening, but that doesn't help us accomplish what we really want."

"And what's that?"

"To draw Fazil out into the open."

"And reporting on this ordeal is going to do just that?" Alex asked. "I fail to see how that will happen."

"Just hear me out," Hawk said. "We know Fazil loves a big show. He's been trying to pull one off back home for years without much success. But here in London, things are different. It's totally possible for him to light up this city on a short notice by activating one of his sleeper cells."

"And why now all of a sudden?" Alex asked.

"Because he finally knows the face of the man who was behind giving the order that killed his little brother. Nothing is going to stop him from getting revenge. And if he can do it on a grander stage with the whole world watching, he will."

"And you think she'll just go for it?" Alex asked.

Hawk nodded.

"Not so fast," Blunt said. "She's already taken this to her editor, apparently."

"So what?"

"Then someone else knows. We can't just deal with this in our usual manner and lean on the editorial board to intervene for us."

"Appeal to the reporter in her," Hawk said. "Sell her on the big story that nobody knows or has right now."

"Davenport is gonna kill us," Alex said.

Hawk nodded. "It's definitely going to piss him off, but he'll appreciate this in the end, especially after Karif Fazil is dead."

"It's worth a shot," Blunt said.

Hawk stood. "Well, we'll give you some privacy then. You have a call to make."

CHAPTER 11

London, England

FAZIL HOVERED OVER a map and studied all the possible exit points. One of the things he appreciated about the west was how available every building plan and schematic was to the public. Charting out a village in the hills of Afghanistan—or even in Kabul—required access to a high-powered satellite. But a person could find practically anything they wanted on the internet or simply by making a request with a governing body.

He marked several points where his men could go if the situation turned south and then stepped back with satisfaction.

They will have to get lucky to catch us.

A knock on the door broke his satisfied gaze. He turned to see one of his assistants holding up a phone.

"You need to see this," he said.

Fazil took the phone and started reading a news

story from *The Washington Post* about the kidnapping of Davenport's family. He growled as he scanned the article.

"It's everywhere now," the assistant said. "Newspapers, television, internet. There isn't a single outlet anywhere that doesn't have that story on the front page."

Fazil picked up one of the wooden chairs and slung it, splintering it against the far wall of his office. He paced around and mumbled to himself about Davenport making a grave mistake.

"Should I call the others for an emergency meeting?" the assistant asked.

Fazil nodded. "Fifteen minutes. Right here."

The assistant scurried away, leaving Fazil alone to contemplate his next move. He had wanted to handle everything discreetly until he was ready to make a public show of killing Davenport. But Davenport didn't follow the rules. There would be consequences. Fazil always made sure there were consequences for ignoring his instructions.

It took less than ten minutes for his office to fill up with advisors and cell leaders. Evana Bahar was the last person to enter the room.

Fazil forced a smile and nodded at her. "Nice of you to join us, *cousin.*"

Bahar didn't react, remaining stoic as she clasped

her hands and placed them on the table in front of her. "I'm here to help figure out how we're going to maneuver discreetly now that everyone knows what we're up to."

"If you think Davenport was keeping this a secret, you're a fool."

She shrugged. "The whole world didn't know before, but apparently, they do now. It puts a fly in our ointment."

"That's why we're getting new ointment."

Fazil stepped back from the table and paced around the room as he unveiled his new plan in light of their private kidnapping being made public.

"We are still moving forward with the plan," he said. "We will have to make some minor tweaks, but the heart of our mission hasn't changed and doesn't need to change, even though everyone knows. They may all be waiting for what's coming next, but they won't be able to react to it until it's too late."

"I disagree," one of the cell leaders said. "There will be more people waving cameras around, looking for us. Even if this information is now public, can't we still handle everything privately?"

"Yes," another advisor agreed. "Let's just drop his body in the Thames, treating him like a commoner. It would be further humiliation."

Fazil held up his hand. "There are numerous

options we hold since we still have the family. But we can make this all work to our benefit instead of completely changing our plans."

"Our plans will be meaningless if we get caught," another advisor chimed in.

"We're not going to get caught. But we are going to move in the opposite direction of what they might expect. In light of this public revelation about the Davenport family abduction, they are trying to force the issue. They think everyone will be looking for us now, that we won't be able to move them without raising suspicion. But as you know, we have no intention of keeping them for very long."

"So, what is the plan?" another cell leader asked. "Our team is already asking."

"The plan is the same as it has always been with one exception—the entire operation will be carried out in broad daylight."

"That's impossible," groused one man.

"The door is that way," Fazil said, gesturing toward the exit. "Feel free to leave at any time. For those of you who are interested in raising the profile of our jihadist organization and advancing our crusade against these barbarians from the west, please stay. You will share in the glory of the strike we are about to deliver to this city."

No one moved, not even the dissenter.

"Now that we've cleared that all up, let's look at the details that are changing."

Fazil spent the next half hour outlining the new direction for Al Hasib's attack. When he finished, he crossed his arms and scanned the room, nodding subtly with a faint smile.

"If they want a show, we're going to give them a show they'll never forget," he said. "Now, where is our hacker friend? We need another favor."

CHAPTER 12

Ministry of Defense Whitehall
London, England

THE NEXT MORNING, Liam Davenport stormed into his office with a copy of *The Times* tucked under his arm. He slammed the newspaper onto his desk and kicked his chair. His assistant, Melissa, poked her head in the door.

"Sir, would you care for a cup of tea?" she asked, holding out a mug.

"As long as you have some brandy to go along with it," he said.

She scrunched up her nose and shook her head. "Sorry, I only bring that in on Fridays."

Her humor broke the tension for a moment. Davenport cracked a smile and gestured for her to place the tea on his desk.

"Sorry," he said. "I'm a little nervous about today."

"That's understandable, sir. I'm sure it will all work out. You'll get Evelyn and the children back soon."

Davenport repositioned his chair beneath his desk and sat down. "There are no guarantees. I should've taken action sooner. Selfishly, I wanted to see them one more time. Now, I may never see them again."

"Keep your chin up, sir. You're due for a bit of good luck."

Davenport shook his head and grabbed the cup of tea. He took a sip before responding. "I hope you're right."

He watched Melissa exit the room, closing the door behind her. Standing up, he cradled the mug with both hands and paced around, weighing his options in light of the kidnapping now becoming a major news story overnight.

Who would've leaked this to the press?

He glanced at his watch, one hour before everyone would reconvene to talk about the plan for later that day. Fazil had kept Davenport in the dark about when the exchange was supposed to occur, but he anticipated finding out soon. Davenport would need enough time to prepare, and Fazil had to be aware of that—unless he didn't care and this was all a charade. Davenport couldn't be sure what was happening, but he was ready for everything to end one way or another.

* * *

DAVENPORT'S PHONE BUZZED just before he stepped into the conference room. He lingered in the hallway to digest the words on the screen.

Midnight. London Bridge. You for your family. No tricks or everyone dies.

He strode into the meeting, opening the proceedings by pounding his fist into the table.

"There are only a handful of people outside of this room who knew what was going on until a report in an American newspaper broke overnight," Davenport said. "I know I'm not likely to get a straight answer from any of you, but I need to know who did this. And I need to know right now."

J.D. Blunt, who had taken up his seat against the wall, raised his hand.

"I take full responsibility for that," Blunt said. "Sorry about the blindside, but I knew you'd never go for it. Yet it had to be done."

"*Had to be done*? Are you out of your mind? As it stands now, we've lost all trust we had with Karif Fazil, who asked us to keep this quiet. Think he's going to do that a second time?"

Blunt held up his hands. "Just calm down for a moment and let me explain."

"Calm down? Me? It's not your family tied up with a psychopath right now in God knows where doing God knows what to them. So please pardon my anxious behavior, will you?"

Blunt persisted. "It was a strategic move. I thought you'd understand."

"How the hell am I supposed to understand when you go around doing bloody well whatever you please without consulting the person whose family is not only at the center of this hostage crisis but is also the leader of the this country's defenses? Please explain that to me because I don't understand any of your moves right now. I brought you here to help us in this process, not screw everything up."

"You're right," Blunt said. "I probably should've spoken with you about this so you weren't so caught off guard."

"How about you should've discussed this with me first before making an unilateral decision?"

"Would you have agreed the idea?" Blunt asked.

"Absolutely not."

"Then now you see why I didn't discuss it with you. I know you might think this sounds crazy right now, but it'll make more sense once I have the opportunity to explain."

"Out with it then. Explain yourself, Senator."

Blunt stood and walked to the center of the

room. He scanned the audience of British dignitaries and leaders before continuing. "If there's anything we've learned about Karif Fazil since we've been tracking him, it's that he loves an audience. When he decides to do something in the shadows, everyone is in danger. The notion that we can sit back and meet his demands in the darkness is misguided and will put your family in greater danger."

"Yet leaking word to the press about what he has done will change all that?" Davenport said with a growl.

"The locations he's aimed attacks at in the U.S. suggest that he's very much interested in making a splash in the news. Hell, he even tried to have Air Force One shot down. But that's not the route he took this time. Fazil has made this operation very personal and private. Yet by leaking this story, the press has taken this scheme in a surprisingly different direction. Since it's public, he'll want to show everyone that he is *the man* and that he can deliver even when every eye is on him."

One of the other advisors shifted in his seat and raised his hand.

Blunt nodded toward him. "Yes?"

"What makes you think he's going to embrace the direction this operation has gone? At one time, this was a simple exchange. Now, it's turned into so much more," the man said.

Davenport sighed and held up his phone. "I haven't even told the senator here this yet, but right before the meeting, I received a text from an unidentified number. It was Fazil. He set the time and place for the exchange—and it's very public."

Blunt's eyebrows shot up as he read the text. "See, there's no need to antagonize me. Let's just figure out the best plan of action."

Davenport read the text aloud as the details sank in with the rest of the leaders around the table. Fazil was not only embracing the aspect that this story was now public and trending all over the world, he was going to make a public spectacle out of it.

"London Bridge?" Admiral Riley said with a whistle. "We're looking at a bunch more dead bodies floating in the Thames."

"It doesn't have to be that way," Davenport said. "I've been thinking about this ever since I heard that Evelyn and the children had been taken by Al Hasib. I'm willing to meet his demands."

Hawk blurted out his objection. "You can't do that, sir. We must remain leery of every promise Fazil makes."

"But aren't you the one who told me this is about a personal vendetta, not jihad? And Fazil has made it very clear how much revenge means to him."

"That doesn't mean he won't try to leave his

mark in other ways. Look, it's the perfect cover for razing London. We're all distracted by his obsession with you that we lose our focus for a moment and get blindsided in a way that will take years to recover, both psychologically not to mention physically and financially. This could be your 9/11 moment."

Davenport interlocked his fingers behind his head and looked up at the ceiling. The pressure to get this right was enormous, both personally and for the country he swore to defend.

"If you're not planning on making the exchange, how do you intend on getting my family back safely?" Davenport asked.

"I'll go in your place," Hawk said.

Davenport scowled. "They'll know it's not me."

"Not if I look like you," Hawk said. "You'd be surprised what a good makeup artist can do."

"But what if they figure you out? They'll kill you. They might even kill my whole family on the spot."

"That's still a possibility even if you went," Hawk countered. "Remember, Fazil wants revenge for the killing of his family members. And I don't want to sound insensitive to you by saying this, but he might have something else in mind for them. Quite honestly, I'll be surprised if he even brings them to the exchange."

Davenport sighed. "Any other input on this idea

of using Mr. Brady Hawk here as my stand-in?"

"I think it could work," Admiral Riley said. "If anyone knows Fazil and his way of thinking in this room, it's Mr. Hawk. He also could stand up to Fazil better in a fight than you would."

Davenport nodded. "You'll get no argument from me there. Anyone else?"

A few other leaders weighed in, including both the MI5 and MI6 directors, who volunteered to help transform Hawk into Davenport. The heads of the security organizations both felt that Hawk would have the best chance of surviving any torture as well as helping British intelligence identify Al Hasib's hideout in the city.

"I doubt Fazil will take me anywhere close to his secret facility, if anywhere at all," Hawk said. "He might try to shoot me right there on the spot."

"In that case, we need to be ready for immediate retribution," Davenport said. "We need to create a perimeter around London Bridge and set up snipers on every rooftop. The good thing is there won't be much pedestrian traffic at that time of night, but we need to make sure people don't get anywhere near the bridge."

Davenport turned toward several of his strategists. "I want an actionable plan on my desk in two hours. Gentlemen, keep all of your men on standby in case this escalates. If all goes right, we can end this thing tonight and put Karif Fazil down in the process."

Davenport dismissed everyone, remaining alone in the conference room.

He wasn't thrilled with the plan, even though it was likely their best chance of getting his family back. But the part that he hated the most was what had been bugging him from the moment Al Hasib stole away with Evenlyn, Ava, Benjamin, and Millie: Davenport wasn't in control. And there was no real way to take back control.

But he considered that was perhaps another way to handle the situation.

CHAPTER 13

KARIF FAZIL CHECKED HIS WATCH and threw his head back, drinking in the cool breeze blowing along the Thames. A light rain started to fall, but Fazil didn't mind. He appreciated the winter season, even though everyone in the western world seemed to despise it. The nip in the air struck quite the contrast from the consistent heat blazing across most of the Middle East no matter what time of year it was.

With the change of plans, he considered all his available options for transporting Evelyn and the children to London Bridge. Davenport wouldn't be so foolish to try and have his snipers take a shot. Fazil figured the intelligence community would advise Davenport to use caution if past history was any indication. Despite all the failed attempts, Fazil had avoided being captured. He always had a backup, a way out to guarantee his safety. By now, he had distilled the protocol down to a simple formula, though he always tried to throw a new wrinkle in just so he wouldn't become too predictable. His life depended on his ability to remain an enigma to those tracking him. But British intelligence and others were likely well versed in Fazil's methods. To challenge him would result in at least one fatality, possibly more depending on how things went down, that much Fazil made sure of. And that was a result Davenport would categorically reject.

One of Fazil's men navigated the boat close to a makeshift dock. A pair of terrorists climbed out of the boat and secured it to an old pylon and then led the family up a flight of stone stairs.

Fazil helped Evelyn out last, holding on to her until they reached the street level. He cinched her suicide vest, jerking her to the left then right. Tears streamed down Evelyn's face, dripping onto Fazil's hand. He looked directly at her and smiled.

"It'll all be over with soon enough," he said. "No need to cry."

He double-checked all the explosives, ensuring everything was connected properly. The vest was bright blue, barely visible due to all the charges draped over almost every inch. When he was satisfied that everything was in working order, he nudged her with the barrel of his gun.

"Let's go catch up with your children," said Fazil, who grinned as he noticed the bridge was blocked off to traffic on both ends. The stage he'd been hoping for since Davenport turned this game on its head had materialized better than imagined.

After a second firm poke, Evelyn complied with Fazil's instructions, sniffling as she turned along the pedestrian path and walked toward the center of the bridge. Fazil watched her eyes widen as she realized what was happening.

"They're going to shoot you," she said, regaining her composure.

"They will try," Fazil said. "They always do."

"My husband won't stand for this," she said. "He's coming for you."

"He may try, but he's going to fail, just like all the others before him."

Evelyn's grief turned to anger. She clenched her fists and gritted her teeth. "You have his family," she said. "He won't miss."

"One small point you need to correct," Fazil said with a smile. "I have four escape cards—you and your three children. If anything happens to me, you all die. They know that. I know that. So, any attempts to rescue them from my care would be like signing their death warrant. He knows better than to test me that way—at least, I hope he does. And you better hope so, too."

She sneered at him and trudged along the bridge

where her children were already standing with more than a dozen agents. Ava started screaming as two Al Hasib agents affixed a harness to her and then lifted her up over the railing above the water.

By the time they made it to the center, Benjamin had also been slung over the bridge, tethered by a network of ropes.

Fazil watched young Millie fight against his agents as she was lowered into position next to Ava, who was in the center. He turned to Evelyn and gestured for her to continue toward the two men who were waiting to fit her with the final harness.

"You're going to burn in hell for this, you know?" Evelyn said as the agents grabbed her arms and pulled them through the web of ropes.

"I'm afraid you're wrong about that," Fazil said. "*You* will be the one who burns in hell, you *infidel*."

Evelyn squirmed and kicked as the men prepared her to be fastened to the front of the bridge.

Fazil walked in front of her and eyed her up and down. "There is only one question left to ask: Do you want to be next to your only son or your youngest daughter?"

Evelyn closed her eyes and shook her head. "You really are a monster."

"I'll take that answer as your son," he said, signaling to the men to finish the job.

They held her over the edge while they tightened the ropes, keeping her just far enough away from Benjamin that she couldn't touch him, despite her relentless efforts. The ropes were wound so tight that her arms started to bleed.

"It doesn't feel good, does it?" Fazil asked mockingly. "At least you will get the freedom you deserve soon enough."

"You said this was going to be an exchange."

Fazil shrugged. "So, I lied."

He turned toward one of his lieutenants. "Do you have him on the line yet?"

"Yes," the man said, handing a phone to Fazil.

"Black Wolf," Fazil said. "I'm so glad you could join us tonight from afar. It's show time."

CHAPTER 14

Ministry of Defense Whitehall
11:15 p.m.

HAWK HAD EXCUSED HIMSELF from the command center for a few minutes to use the restroom. When he returned, the entire chamber was abuzz. Analysts and translators scurried back and forth from desk to desk. Assistants handed out packets of information to the brass seated around an oval-shaped table directly in front of a bank of monitors.

He noticed Blunt seated at the end of the table, chewing on a cigar and whispering something to Alex.

"What did I miss?" Hawk asked.

"Based on the way these people are moving, you'd think the entire earth was about to get obliterated by a giant asteroid," Blunt said.

"That's not funny," Alex said. "I hope you'd spring into action if I was wearing a suicide vest and attached to the front of some international city's landmark bridge."

"I wasn't trying to make light of the situation," Blunt said. "It's just that the British intelligence is notorious for moving slowly."

"And we abide by the shoot-first-ask-questions-later protocol?" Hawk asked.

"That about sums it up," Blunt said.

"Enough of the agency analysis and comparison," Hawk said. "What's happening?"

"As you can see," Alex said, pointing to a screen in the far corner, "the Davenport family is attached snug up against the railing along London Bridge with their feet dangling over the water."

"Well, that's different, even for Fazil," Hawk said.

"He doesn't favor physical torture over psychological torture, that's for sure," Alex said. "That degenerate will get at you any way he can."

Hawk squinted as he studied the screen. He got up out of his chair and moved closer to have a better look.

"Is she wearing what I think she's wearing?" he asked.

"If you think she's wearing a suicide vest, you're right," Blunt said.

"That must be his insurance policy, the way he makes sure to get away," Hawk said. "From what I can tell, that vest looks locked down and wired. He's probably got a password to unlock the vest or unarm the explosives. Either way, it's a good idea."

Alex nodded. "He probably has a detonator, too, in case things go sideways."

"How did they arrive?" Hawk asked.

"By boat," Blunt said. "They used a small fishing boat with twin engines and docked it by the foot of the bridge. But it's gone now."

"Then he must be planning on leaving some other way," Hawk said.

"Let's hope he plans on leaving at all," Alex said. "He could be here for one final stand."

Hawk shook his head. "That's not his style. Fazil wants to be around to revel in his glory. If it looks like he blew himself up, I would bet it was a smokescreen to help him disappear."

Blunt nodded in agreement. "Let's worry about that if we have to. In the meantime, Davenport wants us to analyze this scene and see if we can figure out what Fazil is going to do."

Hawk edged ever closer to one of the screens zooming in on the family members. "I hope they aren't airing this on live television."

"No," Alex said. "Someone told us that was a feed from a nearby television station made at the special request of the staff here. They wanted to be able to monitor everything that was going on."

"Well, my best guess is that he's going to either set off the explosives on Evelyn, killing everyone, or he's going to do something else that we can't see coming this late in the game."

"You better go get ready," she said. "You've only got forty minutes to be down there."

Located just a few blocks away off the Thames, Whitehall was a perfect location to observe everything Fazil had planned that evening. Both the physical proximity as well as the technology necessary to conduct an operation with many moving parts gave the Ministry of Defense a strategic advantage.

Hawk hustled down the hall where a team of makeup artists were waiting for him. They wasted little time in getting his mask in position and attached to Hawk's face. The hair took the longest part as they had to add Davenport's salt-and-pepper look. With fifteen minutes to spare, they finished. Hawk attached the voice box to his chest, enabling him to also sound exactly like Davenport.

"Wow," one of the women said. "If I didn't know any better, I'd swear you were him."

"That's the point, ladies," Hawk said. "Thank you for your excellent work."

Outside, an officer was waiting to shuttle Hawk down to the London Bridge and negotiate. He was oblivious to the panic that had fallen upon the command center while he was being doted over.

* * *

ALEX STUDIED THE SCREEN, noting how similar the Davenport family looked like a gang of insubordinate pirates who used to get tied to the bowsprit of a sailing vessel. Really ruthless captains would leave pirates there as they engaged in battle, resulting in almost sure death. Fazil certainly fit that description, but she was still missing one major detail: How was he going to kill them?

With no ships heading in their direction that could collide with them, the punishment simply seemed to be a form of psychological torture. But she wasn't convinced. And that's when she heard something that arrested her attention.

"We've got some other problems right now," one officer said. "Someone has hijacked one of our drones."

Then it all clicked for Alex.

That's how he's gonna do it.

She rushed over to the officer she'd heard make the announcement that went almost unnoticed in the fever-pitched atmosphere of the war room. "You just said that someone stole one of your drones," she said. "What kind?"

"A Reaper. Why?"

Alex's eyes widened. "I need access to your

mainframe right now. Things are about to get real, if you know what I mean."

"I'm afraid I can't do that right now. I—"

Alex didn't wait around for his bureaucracy spiel. She hustled across the room to Davenport to share her theory. "Sir, I hate to tell you this, but I think I know Fazil's next move."

"Go on."

"I overheard one of your officers say that a weaponized Reaper has just been hacked. I believe Fazil plans to use that to target London Bridge, sir."

Davenport eyed her closely. "You don't think Fazil will honor his word?"

"We warned you that this wasn't about that. He doesn't care if you show up or not. He simply wants to inflict the same pain on you that he endured. He wants you to watch your family die."

"Can you stop this?" he asked.

"I've hacked a Reaper before. I can do it again."

"Do it. Just let me know what you need."

"I need access to your mainframe and a terminal to start working."

Davenport stood on top of a chair. "Everyone, listen up. Things have changed. We believe Al Hasib has stolen a weaponized Reaper and will be flying it straight down the Thames. I need any and all personnel to divert their attention right now to helping Miss

Duncan hack back into the Reaper and regain control of it before it annihilates London. Is that clear?"

Heads bobbed along with a chorus of "yes, sirs" before the hive of activity elevated yet again. In less than thirty seconds, Alex was hammering away on a keyboard, trying to regain control of the drone.

In all the commotion, no one noticed Davenport slip out of the room.

* * *

HAWK LEAPT OUT of the vehicle and hustled down a set of stairs to the water's edge. He wanted to get a better idea of what he was up against before he decided to give himself up and make the exchange. If there was another way—a way to take out Fazil *and* rescue the Davenport family—Hawk wanted to do it. But given the amount of firepower Fazil commanded on the bridge, Hawk quickly realized any deviation was a bad idea.

Hawk worked his way along the trusses, stopping to rest by the piles. His forearms burned, but he ignored the pain as he neared the center. When he reached the closest pile, he craned his neck out from underneath the bridge to get a better perspective. The Davenports were all still in place.

Hawk eased back into the shadows and checked his watch. He hadn't heard any chatter on his earpiece since he was dropped off.

"Can anyone out there let me know what's going on?" Hawk asked. "I've got seven minutes by my watch until midnight."

"Mr. Hawk, this is Sgt. Spiller. There has been a major development that has everyone here busy. Please don't do anything yet. And for the love of god, get away from that bridge."

"What's happened?" Hawk asked.

"Alex wanted me to tell you that Al Hasib has hijacked one of our Reapers, and it's bearing down on your location as we speak."

"How far away is it?"

"Less than two minutes before impact."

"Shit," Hawk said as he started scrambling back toward the shore beneath the trusses. This time he didn't take a break.

"Tell Alex good luck for me," Hawk said.

"I'm not saying anything to her right now," Spiller said. "We're all just watching her and keeping our mouths shut while she works."

"You're in good hands," Hawks said.

He was almost to the edge by the time he finished talking with Spiller. Hawk gripped one of the beams with both hands and started to build momentum, swinging himself back and forth. He didn't think he'd be able to hold on much longer and wanted to make a flying leap for the bank.

Just as he was about to let go, he heard the Reaper screaming around the bend.

Hawk looked down the river and made contact with the aircraft speeding straight toward him. He swung once more and pushed off with all the strength he had left.

* * *

ALEX'S FINGERS FLEW all over the keyboard as she tried to retake the drone from the hacker. Whoever she was battling was good, cutting her off at several passes. It was almost as if he was anticipating her every move.

"Damn it," she said. "I need a new strategy."

"Better make it fast," Admiral Riley said. "Impact is less than a minute."

"I have control of the weapons system at least," she said. "But I still can't fly this thing. The drone could still cause plenty of damage if they decide to crash it into the bridge."

"We can't let that happen," Riley said.

"I know, I know. Just let me think." Alex closed her eyes and racked her brain. She needed a fresh approach, one that wasn't going to get stunted at every turn.

She resumed pecking on the keyboard. A smile started to spread across her face.

"Thirty seconds to impact," Riley said.

"Hang in there," she said. "I've got this."

"Fifteen seconds."

She said nothing, her full attention zeroing in on the keystrokes she needed to make in the next few seconds to regain control of the aircraft.

"Ten," Riley said, beginning a countdown. "Nine, eight, seven . . ."

On the monitor above them, the television station camera picked up the drone that was skimming just above the water as a small wake formed.

Another camera angle that was fixed on the Davenport family showed a resolute Evelyn. She stared into the distance at the drone, not with a look of fear but of determination and courage. She said something and glanced at her children before turning her eyes back down the river.

"Six, five, four . . ."

Alex hit a few more keys and shouted, "Got it."

Taking control, she forced the plane upward, barely clearing London Bridge before disappearing into the night sky.

The room erupted in applause.

Admiral Riley grabbed Alex by the shoulders. "You did it! You did it!"

She smiled amid the cheering and glanced around the room for Davenport.

Where is he?

She continued flying the drone until a pilot who'd been summoned to assist her took over the controls.

Letting out a long breath, she looked back up at the monitors to see what was happening. Technically, there were still a little over four minutes before Fazil's imposed deadline. She wasn't sure he'd stick to it since she'd just thwarted his party.

"Have you seen Davenport?" she asked Riley, who was still grinning from ear to ear.

He scowled as he looked around the room. "I saw him a minute ago. I'm sure he's here somewhere. Or maybe he needed a moment to himself."

"Where's his office?" Alex asked.

"Down the hall and to the right," Riley said before an assistant shoved a cell phone to his ear. "Yes, Mr. Prime Minister, she did it. Disaster averted."

Alex turned to look at the scene as something on one of the monitors caught her eye. She rushed back into the room and stared at a screen on the corner of the wall.

"Can someone put this monitor up on the big screen?"

One of the aides nodded and quickly granted her request.

As soon as everyone had a moment to digest the image, the air went out of the room. A man with his hands raised walked across the bridge. From the other side, Fazil and his men rushed toward the center with their guns trained on the intruder.

She looked at Riley then glanced back up at the screen. "I think we found Davenport."

CHAPTER 15

London Bridge

"ABORT THE MISSION. I repeat, abort the mission," crackled the voice over the comlink in Hawk's ear. He hadn't stopped running since Sgt. Spiller told him to get away from the bridge. But Hawk figured Alex had somehow regained control of the Reaper since there were no missiles launched or explosions lighting up the night sky.

Hawk finally took up a position along the corner of a building just off King William Street. He could still see down the bridge and noticed some activity.

"Talk to me, Spiller. What's happening?"

"It's Davenport. He's on the bridge, offering himself in exchange for his family, just like Al Hasib initially demanded."

"Damn it. Did he not listen to a thing we told him?"

"He can be a bit of an old codger when he wants to be."

"I'm losing this disguise. If Fazil thinks we're messing with him, he won't hesitate to just start shooting."

"Good idea. Just hang tight, and try to keep an eye on what's happening."

* * *

FAZIL PUT HIS HAND on Kareem Khetran's chest, holding him back from charging down the bridge.

"What do you think you're doing?" Fazil asked.

"We're putting an end to this the old fashioned way. We pull Davenport's family back onto the street, shoot them all in the head in front of Davenport, and then cut him so he bleeds out in front of his dead family."

"And what's going to stop them from shooting us now?" Fazil asked. "This is a delicate game we are playing. We must have leverage if we're going to make it out of here alive."

"Are you forgetting about the vest that the wife is wearing?"

"It's only worth something if they think we'll give it to them. The minute they think it's a lost cause, they're going to start shooting. I won't give them that satisfaction."

"So, what's your plan?"

"Let's do this another way," Fazil said with a grin. "We'll even honor the exchange in some ways. But we will still make Davenport pay for his sins."

"And how do you intend to do that?"

"Just watch," Fazil said as he marched toward the center of the bridge.

* * *

DAVENPORT SCRATCHED around the bottom of the bulletproof vest he donned before going against every piece of advice he'd received since the moment of the kidnapping. In the back of his mind, he figured this would be the end of his job, but he didn't care. The rest of his life would lose meaning if Evelyn and the children were dead. He could find another job somewhere. At least he wouldn't be a coward.

He raised his hands and walked slowly toward his family. He could hear them still screaming for help. During battle, he'd been in some harrowing situations but none as helpless as his family was likely feeling. They'd just seen a Reaper loaded with missiles buzz them and had no idea if Fazil was just playing mind games with them and the drone was about to come around for another shot or if the drone was supposed to be there. They were still tethered to bridge as fearful as ever as evidenced by their cries for help.

"I'm coming," Davenport said.

More cries and screams.

He kept walking, his hands raised in the air.

"Come and take me," Davenport said. "Honor

your word, Mr. Fazil. I'm here. It's midnight. Time to let my family go."

Davenport swallowed hard as he watched Fazil and several guards head toward him, weapons aimed at the ground.

Davenport waited, swallowing hard as he realized that he had no control over what might happen next. Snipers dotted the surrounding rooftops, undoubtedly with the Al Hasib agents in their sights. But they wouldn't pull the trigger unless he gave them the command. That was the agreement. He could only hope no one had an itchy finger and that they did a better job of following orders than he did.

"Mr. Defense Secretary, I know you have an earpiece in," Spiller said. "Can you hear me?"

"Yes, I can," Davenport said.

"Good. Now, don't do anything stupid."

"It's too late for that."

Fazil stopped a few meters away. "Tell your snipers to stand down, then we'll talk."

Davenport passed along the instructions, and he watched as the snipers dipped back into the shadows out of plain view.

"A little trust goes a long ways," Fazil said.

"And trust must go both ways," Davenport said. "You said you wanted me for my family. Please honor your word."

Fazil gestured for his men to pull over Davenport's wife and children. Within a couple minutes, they were all tugged back over the railing and safely on solid ground.

Davenport glowered as he stared at the vest strapped to his panicked wife.

"Take that off her now," Davenport said.

Fazil furrowed his brow. "You're not in charge any more. That vest is our insurance that we get out of here. Once we are safely away, I will send the code to someone to remove the vest."

"How do I know I can trust you?" Davenport asked.

"How do you know you can trust anyone? We must crawl before we can walk; at least that's what you say in the west. Right now, we are crawling. You do one thing for me; I do one thing for you. Do we understand each other?"

Davenport nodded. He took a few steps toward Evelyn before a pair of Al Hasib agents stepped in his way.

"What do you think you're doing?" Fazil asked. "This is not the reunion episode of a reality show. I don't know what you might pass her, so we're going to prohibit any physical touching right now."

Davenport looked at his children. Millie was calling for him.

"Father," she said, reaching toward him between her hysterical sobs. "I'm scared."

"It's all right, sweetie. Just keep holding your sister's hand. Everything is going to be fine."

"No, it's not," Millie said. "They're going to beat you like they did Mom, and then they're going to kill you."

Davenport fought back tears. He needed to show his family strength and give them some semblance of hope. "We're just going to work a few things out," he said. "Don't worry."

"No! Don't leave us!"

Fazil motioned for his men to put the Davenport family in an SUV that had just rolled up. "It's time to say goodbye," Fazil said. "And you can do it from right where you're standing."

"Stay strong, Evelyn," Davenport said. "It's going to be okay."

Davenport watched the bright-red taillights dim as the car drove across the bridge where a tactical team had assembled.

"I'll give them the code once I know we're safe," Fazil said.

One of the Al Hasib agents ziptied Davenport's hands behind him and led him to the vehicle waiting on the bridge. Fazil got in the front passenger seat and motioned for the rest of his entourage to exit the bridge.

* * *

ALEX'S SHORT-LIVED CELEBRATION at Whitehall was replaced by even more frantic activity and hand wringing by the various department leaders in the room. She sat back down at her terminal and took a deep breath before adjusting her ear piece.

"You should be able to speak with agent Hawk," Spiller said. "I know he's listening."

"Yeah, I'm here," Hawk said. "And I'm watching the vehicle with the Davenport family drive straight toward me. What the hell was he thinking?"

"He wasn't thinking," Alex said. "And neither were we. Nobody realized he was missing until it was too late."

"Well, we still have some work to do," Hawk said. "I'm sure you saw that Evelyn was still wearing that suicide vest. You need to separate her from everyone else as soon as possible. I don't trust Fazil."

"I'm on it," Spiller said over the coms.

"What do you think you should do now?" Alex asked. "There's not much you can do out there since everyone is gone."

"I want to track Fazil and Davenport, but I think you're best suited to do that. I'll head back over there. Keep me apprised of any new developments."

"Roger that."

Alex returned her attention to the bank of

monitors. A member of the MI5 technical staff was shuffling the images on the wall, replacing any of the London Bridge images with closed-circuit TV feeds.

"He's going to have a hard time escaping us," Admiral Riley said. "This city is wired to track any- and-everyone."

"I hope you're right," Alex said. "The Defense Secretary's life just might depend on it."

Less than a minute later, the screens began to go dark.

"What's happening?" Alex asked as a murmur spread among the onlookers.

"I don't know," the MI5 tech said. "Someone is killing these feeds."

"When did Al Hasib get savvy enough to start pulling off these kinds of technical feats?" Spiller asked.

Alex shook her head. "I'm not sure, but there aren't but a handful of hacks able to steal a drone and systematically take down a city's CCTV feed."

"Who would you suppose this is then?" Spiller pressed.

"My money would be on Black Wolf," Alex said.

"But I thought he was dead."

"Don't believe everything you see. And right now, we can't see a damn thing."

* * *

FAZIL'S GAZE DARTED back and forth as he considered his next move. He was thankful that he built in a large margin for error as well as thought through several contingency plans. If he hadn't, his body would likely be scattered across the Thames.

"Where is he?" Fazil asked one of the men in the back seat next to Davenport.

The man turned and reached behind him. After a few seconds, he faced the front holding Jafar.

"There you are," Fazil said, taking his bird and holding it close to his face. "Sorry you had to miss all the action tonight, little man. But I didn't want anything to happen to you."

"Seriously? You have a pet pigeon?" Davenport asked. "You can't make this stuff up."

"I suggest you keep your mouth shut," Fazil said. "I'm very protective of Jafar."

Fazil shifted in his seat when his phone started ringing. He answered the call. After speaking to one of his agents, he ordered the driver to turn around.

"Go to the meeting location," Fazil ordered.

The driver slowed briefly before spinning the wheel around and zipping off in the opposite direction. After a couple minutes, they parked beneath a bridge and switched vehicles.

"When will you give my wife the code?"

Davenport asked as one of the agents dragged him out of the SUV and shoved him toward the other one.

"When I know that we're safe," Fazil said. "And we're not safe yet."

Once the group was reassembled in the new SUV, they sped away and headed back toward their hideout. Once they reached their destination, a garage door shot upward and several armed guards motioned them inside.

Everyone began to pile out of the vehicle.

"I think you're safe now," Davenport said. "Please honor your word and send my wife the code."

Fazil turned slowly toward his captive. "You sure do make a lot of demands for a man who isn't in the position to make any."

Davenport gave Fazil a steely gaze. "Make the call."

Fazil snatched a phone out of his pocket and handed it to Davenport. "Dial the number."

As Davenport was dialing, Fazil issued a warning. "Put the phone on speaker. Only pass along the code I give you. Don't say anything else. Understand?"

Davenport nodded.

One of the staff in the command center answered the call.

"I need to speak with Sgt. Spiller," Davenport said.

"Mr. Defense Secretary, is that you?" the man asked.

"Spiller, please."

After a few seconds, Spiller answered.

"What the bloody hell were you thinking, sir?" Spiller asked.

"I don't have time to discuss all that. I just called to pass along the code to unlock Evelyn's vest."

"Are you all right?" Spiller asked.

"Do you have a pen and paper handy?"

"Yes."

"Pass along this code to whoever is with Evelyn, and make sure the children are elsewhere in case this is a trap."

"A trap? What kind of trap?"

"Just separate them for this, will you?"

"I will comply. The code, sir?"

Fazil relayed to Davenport, who repeated it back for Spiller. After they were finished, Fazil motioned for Davenport to hand over the phone.

Davenport shook his head. "Not until I know my wife is safe."

Fazil shrugged. "If you insist."

"Sir, I'm going to patch you in to my call," Spiller said.

Fazil smiled wryly and waited.

There was a clicking noise followed by the voice of a man who answered the call.

"This is Sgt. Spiller. I have the code to unlock her vest."

"Go ahead."

"Repeat each number after me so that I know you are entering the correct one."

"Understood."

Spiller started to rattle off the numbers. When he'd finished, he gave the final instruction. "Now, press the pound key."

A high-pitched tone preceded a loud explosion.

"Talk to me," Spiller said. "Are you there?"

Nothing.

Davenport glared at Fazil. "What did you do?"

"Oops. I must have forgotten a number," Fazil said as he snatched the phone from Davenport just before knocking him out.

CHAPTER 16

Ministry of Defense Whitehall

BLUNT TOOK IN THE CHAOS from a seat in the back corner of the room while chewing on his cigar. While he was empathetic toward the plight of the British intelligence community, particularly Davenport, Blunt was relieved this situation wasn't occurring in the streets of Washington or New York City. And he was glad his people weren't directly involved, even though they were working hard to help catch Karif Fazil.

He glanced at his watch. It was approaching 1:00 a.m., and the energy to catch Fazil almost evaporated when the report spread that Evelyn Davenport and a member of the London police department's bomb squad had been killed when her suicide vest exploded. Fortunately, the Davenport children were safe, but the psychological damage had been inflicted, the kind Blunt knew they'd never get over. Such a ruthless act by Fazil made it all the more imperative that they catch him.

Blunt resisted the twinge of guilt he felt coming on over steering the hostage situation in the direction that he did. Fazil was probably going to kill Evelyn all along, even though they'd never know for sure. At least the children were safe, even if there was a good chance they'd all be orphaned by sunrise.

Blunt's phone rang with a call from a familiar Washington number. He wanted to ignore it, but he couldn't. Given the circumstances, he didn't want to gamble that the call was unimportant.

"Miss Youngblood," Blunt said as he answered the call. "Thank you for your assistance in this matter. You've been most helpful."

"Are you sure about that?" she asked. "I'm hearing reports that the British defense minister's wife is now dead. Can you confirm or deny that?"

"I'd prefer that the children hear it first before social media takes over," he said. "Would you mind having the common courtesy of waiting a few hours before publishing that?"

"That's not the world we live in any more, Senator. If it's news, it has to be now. Otherwise, it's relegated to the trash heap of information people already knew twenty minutes ago in their Twitter feed."

Blunt sighed. "Whatever, just don't use my name.

I prefer to be known as a source."

"I can go along with that."

"Thank you," Blunt said. "Your discretion is most appreciated."

"Is this the kind of help you envisioned when you asked me to run that story?"

"Three children are safe and sound thanks to how this situation went down."

"But they're all as good as orphaned now."

"Better than being dead, wouldn't you say?" Blunt said.

"I don't know," she said. "But I am wondering if I should publish my exposé on Firestorm. If your team is over there helping right now and this is the kind of results that you provide, it might be best if Firestorm ceased to exist."

"Watch yourself, Miss Youngblood. You aren't exactly in a position to be making such judgment calls."

"And you aren't in a place to be challenging me."

Blunt took a deep breath and exhaled slowly so he didn't say something he would later regret. "You sound like you might be threatening me," he said. "I won't be subjected to an ongoing blackmail scheme so you can coerce whatever information out of me that you wish."

"I upheld my end of the bargain. Now it's time

that you uphold yours."

"The bargain was that I give you the scoop on the biggest breaking news story in lieu of exposing some alleged black ops group within the U.S. government. I've done that already. If you keep coming back to the well hoping to squeeze out another drop, you just might find yourself at the bottom."

"This quid pro quo between us needs to be stronger. You're getting the far better end of the deal."

Blunt closed his eyes. He wanted to scream. Camille Youngblood was never going to stop milking him for information if he didn't make a grand concession.

"I've got one final story I can help you with, but once it's done, I never want to hear from you again. Understand?"

"I'm not sure I can agree to such a thing. This really depends on what it is."

"The truth about Al Hasib, the behind-the-scenes story of the rise of one of the most deadly terrorist organizations in the world and how it ascended to such power. How does that sound?"

"I think I could go for that," she said.

"Good," Blunt said. "Now if you ever threaten me again, so help me God—"

"You'll what? Have me fired? Silenced? Killed?"

"Don't push your luck," Blunt said before he hung up.

CHAPTER 17

HAWK SLEPT HARD all night despite the fact that everything about the exchange and near miss with the Reaper weighed heavily on his mind. If it hadn't been for Alex, the Reaper could've obliterated London Bridge as well as other parts of the city. There was no reason to think Fazil would've exacted his revenge in other ways as well if he maintained control of the drone.

The challenge looming was how to locate Davenport and bring him home safely. It was a large task that would require weeks of research—unless Hawk could cut to the chase and find the one person who could tell him what was happening among the hardliners in the Muslim community without drawing any suspicion. The situation was already destined to be delicate as it was given that a Muslim-based terrorist organization was claiming full responsibility and promising another show.

Hawk spent most of the day working with Alex to break down everything they could from the footage of the exchange. Alex spoke with the leader of the cyber crimes division from Scotland Yard's Counter Terrorism Command. She debriefed him on everything she noticed during the hijacking of the Reaper as well as the CCTV outage that allowed Fazil and his crew to escape. Meanwhile, Hawk spoke with several MI5 agents about the most likely area in the city that could be cultivating a new generation of terrorists. One of the agents suspected a mosque in Finsbury Park, suggesting that if there was any mosque capable of radicalizing Muslims for jihadist causes, that was the one.

Hawk wanted to check it out immediately, but Alex warned him against it. After getting wind of what Hawk wanted to do, Blunt called one of his friends at the CIA to see what information they had on the mosque, which turned out to be a fortuitous call. The CIA liaison informed Blunt that they had plenty of intel on the mosque and its activities but recommended talking to an agent they had embedded there named Joe Calder. Calder went by Malik in London and gave Blunt an address.

"Be careful talking to him," Blunt said as he handed over the details to Hawk. "We don't want to spook anyone who might be watching him. Just be as discreet as possible."

"Always," Hawk said.

He checked his watch. It was 5:30 p.m., and Hawk decided to grab something to eat before paying Calder a visit.

After dinner, Hawk bypassed Calder's apartment lobby security by following an elderly woman inside and offering to help her with her groceries. Hawk felt a little slimy for his tactic, even though he concluded he likely would've given the lady a hand any way.

Hawk jimmied the lock to get inside before re-securing the door and taking a seat in a chair in the far corner. He sat waiting until around 7:30 p.m. when a key was inserted into the door. Hawk waited until Calder was fully inside before turning on a reading lamp next to the chair.

"What the bloody hell?" Calder said, setting his groceries down. "Who are you? And what are you doing in my house?"

Hawk held up his hands. "I just want to talk, Joe."

"How do you—"

"CIA. They gave me your information because I need to speak with you right now about a serious matter."

Calder turned on the overhead light and then sat on the couch across from Hawk.

"Is this about that incident last night on London Bridge?" Calder asked.

Hawk nodded.

"Well, I can save us both a lot of time. I didn't know anything about it."

Hawk arched his eyebrows. "Nothing at all?"

"Zip. In fact, the mosque I'm a member of has been quite repulsed by all these antics by Al Hasib. At least, that's what the people are saying publicly. And if they're going to think differently, I think they would feel the freedom to say it to one of their own."

"Fair enough."

"If Al Hasib is recruiting terrorists here in London, they aren't doing it at my mosque. Quite frankly, I don't know which mosque they could be doing it at. The handful that lean toward the radical side of things know they're being watched. They know the government is just looking for an excuse to push them out, so there's not a cleric I know who would risk his position and power to do that unless he intended to never come back."

"So, where else could Al Hasib find willing locals?"

"There's one organization I've heard of that has frequent opportunities to recruit from, though I would say these people are likely difficult to turn."

Hawk scooted to the edge of his seat. "How so?"

"ROARS—the Resettlement of Asylum and Refuge Seekers—works directly with displaced people once they arrive in London. Most of their clients are refugees who have just left a war-torn region, and, more often than not, a Muslim one at that. Trying to get these people to participate in a clandestine operation that jeopardizes the very thing they came here for—their freedom—is a monumental task."

"I imagine so. But you still think it's possible, don't you?"

Calder nodded. "I'm going to give you the name of someone there who might be the one who could pull this off. But beware—this group is very leery of outsiders and closes ranks quickly if they think someone is investigating them. Nobody has been able to penetrate them so far to look further into some of the suspicions the MI5 and other intelligence agencies hold about this organization. But you might get lucky."

Hawk thanked Calder for the information and slipped into the hallway before easing down the stairwell.

When Hawk reached the street, he glanced at the name on the piece of paper.

This ought be interesting.

He called Alex.

"I need you to do me a favor," Hawk said.

"Fire away."

"I need everything you can get me on a non-profit called ROARS, the Resettlement of Asylum and Refuge Seekers."

"I'm on it."

CHAPTER 18

DAVENPORT WANTED TO CLOSE his eyes and awake to the reality that everything he had just experienced was simply a bad dream. But he couldn't even close his eyes. An Al Hasib guard used a device to keep Davenport's eyelids from blinking without inflicting pain. The thought of trying to sleep while enduring such torture wasn't an option he seriously considered.

Compounding the physical pain was the psychological agony. Unless Fazil was utilizing some trick, Evelyn was gone. Davenport wanted to grieve. He would've settled for simply crying. But he couldn't. The fight to stay alive was still in him if only to make sure that his children weren't orphaned by the time this ordeal was over.

Davenport looked around his dank cell. Mold grew on the wall. A stench that smelled like a cross between rotting meat and spoiled milk burned in his nose. Each deep breath was painful as his hands were chained high above his head. With his shoes removed, his feet felt frozen due to the standing pool of water at his feet.

Without any outside light in his cell, he couldn't tell what time of day it was, much less what day of the week. He didn't think he'd been here that long, but each minute felt like an hour. The thought of Millie, Benjamin, and Ava scared and alone terrified him more than anything. Would they remember their father as a foolish and reckless man whose decision orphaned them? Or would they think of him as a courageous hero, willing to do anything to save his family?

He didn't want to dwell on what his legacy would be. There were so many things he could've done differently, yet no one would know his biggest mistake.

If I hadn't been so selfish in wanting to see them before they left . . .

That notion alone was more painful than anything Fazil could do to Davenport, psychologically or physically.

The door to his cell creaked as it opened, and a pair of guards stormed inside and unchained him. They handed him some water and bread. When he finished, they slid a bucket into the corner and told him if he needed to relieve himself, this was his chance. When Davenport finished, the guards commenced to beating him for several minutes. He could feel the blood mixed with sweat trickling down his face. His whole body throbbed with pain.

One of the guards rolled Davenport him onto his side and kicked him in the gut twice more before inserting his hands into the chains and returning him to his place against the wall. Davenport moaned and asked for more water. The two men laughed before slamming the door shut and locking it.

The dim fluorescent bulb hummed, creating a torturous soundtrack on its own. The only respite from the noise came when the light flickered.

Davenport took a deep breath, wincing as he did. He needed to calm down and regain his wits. Wallowing in self-pity was never what he intended to do. The pain of losing Evelyn had overwhelmed him, surprising him at just how deep the hurt was. He bet on Fazil wanting to capture the British Secretary of Defense more than simply inflicting pain on him. But Davenport had bet wrong. Yet the game wasn't over. He just needed to focus and execute what he'd come here to do. His plan was still very much alive.

Davenport could only guess how much time had passed since he'd heard footsteps down the hall when the guards last visited his cell. Two hours, maybe three. But it didn't matter. The important thing was that Davenport had managed to block out the pain and zero in on executing step one.

A guard stepped into the room, followed by Fazil with Jafar seated on his shoulder.

"Mr. Davenport, I hope you've found your accommodations here suitable," Fazil said with a smile. "You're our first guest."

Davenport didn't flinch. He glared at Fazil.

"It hurts, doesn't it?" Fazil asked.

"I'm not sure what you're referring to."

"The pain of losing someone you love. It's difficult."

Davenport shrugged. "I haven't really had any time to think about it."

"So, what have you been thinking about while you've been holed up in this luxurious space?"

"How I'm going to kill you."

Fazil laughed. "I never would've taken someone like you to be into fantasy, but if that's what you're thinking about, I would assume as much."

"You'd be wrong. My thoughts are very much grounded in reality."

"Well, you'd better hurry because I have some special plans for us."

Davenport shook his head. "I'm not interested."

"I'm not asking. But don't worry. I'll be back soon."

Fazil spun on his heels and then headed toward the door.

"And Karif?"

Fazil turned around slowly. "Yes?"

"I'm going to roast that bird of yours on a spit."

Fazil laughed again. "You're not exactly in any

position to be making such threats."

Fazil rushed toward Davenport and delivered a vicious blow to his gut. Davenport groaned as he absorbed the hit.

"You'll be thinking about me as you die, wishing you'd never ordered that Reaper to destroy my family," Fazil said. "Your children will never be safe again."

He turned and exited the room, the door creaking behind him and the guard as they left.

Davenport waited until they were down the hall before he let out a long moan. His whole stomach throbbed as he tried to fight through the pain.

Just give me one guard. That's all I need.

Two hours passed, and Davenport got his wish. A guard checked on Davenport, allowing him to use the restroom and giving him a small cup of water.

Davenport asked to relieve himself in private. The guard rolled his eyes.

"Afraid I'm going to tell everyone about your—"

"Where's your partner?" Davenport interrupted.

"Did you miss him? He'll be back during our next round. I didn't know you were that friendly with one another."

"I would choose my words carefully if I were you," Davenport warned.

Hunched over the bucket, Davenport scratched feverishly at a fresh scab on his left forearm. After a

154 | R.J. PATTERSON

few seconds, he managed to peel it back and dug just beneath the surface to pull out a small razor blade.

When Davenport was finished, he returned to his spot against the wall.

"Give me your arm," the guard commanded.

Davenport hoisted his left arm up, revealing the bloody forearm. The guard gawked at the blood oozing downward.

"What happened here?" he asked.

Davenport used his right hand to slash horizontally across the guard's throat, severing his jugular. In less than a minute, he was dead.

Davenport held his foot up against the guard's and smiled.

Just my luck. We wear the same size shoe.

Davenport eased his feet into the guard's shoes before snatching the gun off him. After a brief search of the man's body, Davenport didn't find anything else of interest. Unfortunately, there wasn't even a cell phone available.

The gun will have to do.

Davenport blotted his forearm by tearing off a piece of the guard's shirt then crept into the hallway, peering in both directions. Davenport had no idea of where he was, but that didn't matter.

He didn't plan on going down in a cell somewhere. He was going to fight.

CHAPTER 19

ALEX ACCOMPANIED HAWK to the ROARS office to investigate Calder's claims. They decided to pose as journalists from *The Washington Post,* writing a story on refugees resettling in Europe. Alex worked quickly to create some phony business cards to help legitimize themselves should the need arise. She also created a pair of identification badges for Carl Templeton and Bianca Thurman.

Hawk looked at the badges before they entered the building. "Templeton and Thurman, huh? That sounds like some buddy cop show."

"Or a law firm or mortuary."

Hawk smiled. "I like the alliteration. It's a nice touch."

"Better than Hawk and Duncan."

"I'm not sure about that."

"Never mind all that," she said. "Time to get to work."

Hawk opened the door, holding it for his partner.

They chose to stop by late in the afternoon after most of the organization's traffic had subsided, at least according to an app on her iPhone. After 3:00 p.m., the place looked to be a virtual ghost town.

"Hi, miss," Alex said as she approached the receptionist's desk. The woman sitting behind the counter wore a hijab and barely made eye contact with them before looking away.

"May I help you?" the receptionist asked.

"I'm hoping so," Alex said. "Bianca Thurman with *The Washington Post*. My colleague Carl Templeton and I are working on a freelance piece about refugees resettling across Europe, and we were wondering if we might be able to speak with your founder, Miss Evana Bahar. We only need about fifteen minutes of her time."

The woman nodded. "Let me check."

She picked up her phone and pressed a single button. She held up her index finger, signaling for them to wait.

"Miss Bahar, there are a couple of reporters who want to speak with you about a story on refugees."

A muffled response.

"They're freelance writers for *The Washington Post*."

A loud, high-pitched noise emanated from the receiver. "She'll see you now," the woman said. "Please, follow me."

Hawk glanced at the family seated in a row against the back wall, awaiting assistance. Everyone had a dark complexion and appeared to be of Middle Eastern descent. They served as a brief reminder why Firestorm was necessary. Families getting displaced due to all the regional and sectarian violence gnawed at him. Despite the pleasant look on their faces, Hawk could tell the people would rather be back in their homeland than trying to start a new life in a foreign place that wasn't as friendly to Muslims. That's how it always was. If there was no violence, they would rather raise their family in familiar surroundings where a close-knit network of family and friends existed. London might as well be another planet to them.

Hawk followed the receptionist and Alex down a long corridor that stopped in front of Bahar's office at the end. The receptionist knocked and was welcomed inside. She introduced Hawk and Alex as Carl Templeton and Bianca Thurman, respectively. Without another word, the receptionist vanished into the hallway, pulling the door shut.

Bahar was busily typing on her computer, yet to look up at her guests.

"I'm almost done," she said as her fingers flew.

"Take your time," Alex said.

"There," Bahar said. "I'm all yours—for now." She glanced at her watch. "I've got almost fifteen minutes exactly, but I hear that's all you need. Correct?"

Alex nodded. "We just have a few questions as we're gathering this story for The Post."

"Let's get right to it," Bahar said, inviting Hawk and Alex to sit in the chairs across from her desk. "What do you want to know?"

"We have a few questions about how things work, starting with the process of how you determine which refugees and asylum seekers to help," Alex asked.

Bahar's eyes widened. "You really have dispensed with the small talk, haven't you?"

Alex forced a smile.

"Well then," Bahar said. "I guess I'll jump right in and try to answer this one for you."

Bahar droned on for a few minutes about their selection protocol and how they decided who to help and who to turn away.

Alex interjected periodically with a "that's interesting" or "that's fascinating" or "I never knew that." But that didn't distract Bahar. She kept right on talking.

After a few more questions, Alex realized Bahar didn't really have anywhere to go. Either that or she enjoyed divulging everything about what they were doing. Or it could've been a combination of the two. Regardless, the final result was a long-winded explanation.

Not that Alex cared. Her job was simple, as was Hawk's. Pretend to be journalists and plant a bug on her.

Alex carried out the main thrust of their mission, attaching a tracker to Bahar so they could follow her movements and see if it would lead back to Fazil's secret hideout. It was a long shot, but something Hawk was confident he could find if his services were required to hunt her down. Alex showed interest in a framed photograph that had been enlarged behind Bahar's desk. When Alex asked to step around to inspect it closer, she placed her hand on Bahar's back and slid the tracker into her collar.

A few more poignant questions about the biggest issues facing refugees today in both their settlement and adjustment into a western world that has grown increasingly fearful of Muslim filled up the quarter hour they requested and then some. When Bahar finished talking, she shook their hands and smiled.

"Stories like the one you are writing assist us greatly in our cause," Bahar said. "Without journalists sharing the accounts of these refugees and what they go through, the world may not ever know just what kind of trials these people endure on their journey to freedom and peace."

Hawk offered his hand. "Glad to help."

She escorted them down the hall and to the lobby.

"Can I get your cards?" Bahar asked. "If I think

of something that might be helpful, I want to be able to contact you."

"Sure," Alex said, digging a card out from the bottom of her purse. "If you think of something, feel free to give me a call or email me."

"I will," Bahar said.

They waited to talk until they reached the street.

"Where does that phone go to?" Hawk asked.

"A dummy line I set up," Alex said. "Goes straight to voicemail. But it does allow me to track back any calls that are made to it."

"Good work," Hawk said. "When Blunt says he only hires the best in the business, I know he's not just blowing smoke."

"So, what's your gut telling you?" she asked.

"I had a hard time getting a read on her. She seemed very passionate about her work, but there was something there. I'm not sure what it was. It could've been that she just doesn't trust journalists."

"She seemed open in her responses."

"Her body language said otherwise, but I guess we'll wait and see where she goes."

* * *

EVANA RETURNED TO HER OFFICE and finished typing an email before pulling the card out of her pocket. She studied the names for a moment before deciding to enter them into Google. The first

two searches that came up for each of them were
LinkedIn profiles showing their employment to be
The Washington Post. She also located a couple of
articles from each of them, all about displaced people.
A couple of the stories focused on the United
Nations' exploits to help shoulder the burden of the
large resettlement camps in various nations. There was
also a story on why Middle Eastern countries refused
to help their own.

Everything seemed to line up with their purported credentials, but she couldn't shake the nagging
feeling of uneasiness. If they were freelancers for *The
Washington Post*, wouldn't they have plenty of articles
with their byline attached in that publication? But
nothing. And wouldn't they write on something else
at least once. She decided to put her suspicions to the
test and dialed *The Washington Post* newsroom. She
talked to a couple of editors, neither of which had
heard of a Templeton or Thurman. But both editors
reiterated that it meant nothing. They dealt with scores
of freelance journalists all the time, and the chances
of remembering one offhand was unlikely.

Evana hung up, still unconvinced. She glanced at
the card again with Bianca Thurman's name embla-
zoned across the front.

"You'll be getting a call all right," she said. "But
it won't be from me."

CHAPTER 20

FAZIL STUDIED HIS BLOODIED knuckles before gesturing for one of his men to bring him a towel. Jafar bounced around on the table in front of him before flitting around the room. With patience and persistence, Fazil cleaned his hands. He then dug deep into a bag of seeds and held it out for his bird. Jafar fluttered up and perched on Fazil's wrist, occupying the perfect location to begin a feeding frenzy.

"The men are ready," an aide reported.

"Tell them I'm on my way," Fazil said as he stroked Jafar's head. "You eat up because we have a big night ahead of us. We're going to get the men prepared for one of the biggest moments of their lives."

Fazil climbed up onto a makeshift stage comprised of wooden shipping pallets piled in the center of the warehouse. He strutted around for a few seconds as the men gathered chanted his name.

Soaking in the moment, he surveyed the crowd and was pleasantly surprised at its size. During his most recent conversation about the number of volunteers who had signed up for the mission, he barely had enough to pull it off. But now he had a full-fledged army, more than triple the number of people.

"Fa-zil! Fa-zil! Fa-zil!" they chanted.

He pumped his fist and nodded before abruptly holding up both hands in a gesture to silence the mass.

"Thank you all for coming tonight and for volunteering to be a part of this event that will long be remembered in the history books as the night of terror in London. After we are through, your names will be immortalized, like the names of those 19 hijackers who flew their planes into those iconic American landmarks on 9/11."

The chant re-started. "Fa-zil! Fa-zil! Fa-zil!"

"Now, I know that we're all excited about the opportunity to demonstrate our loyalty to Islam, our passion for jihad, and our thirst for revenge. Tomorrow night, the people who have waged an unjust war against our countries will pay the ultimate price. There will also be innocent bystanders who will lose their lives in the same way that many of us have witnessed innocent loved ones spill blood for simply being in the wrong place at the wrong time. They will all soon know what it feels like to be attacked in the most vicious of ways without any way to stop it."

More chanting. Fazil waited until the crowd stopped before continuing.

"What we're about to do tomorrow night isn't about you. It isn't about me. It's about giving a voice to our fallen brothers and sisters, fathers and brothers, cousins and uncles, and aunts and nieces and nephews. It's about striking a blow at the heart of a country who claims to exercise a form of democratic government at home while acting like a tyrant abroad. Tomorrow night, we will show them what tyranny looks like, and they will be very afraid!"

Everyone in attendance erupted. Fazil quickly realized he had amped up the crowd to the point that he wouldn't get them back any time soon. And he was fine with that. He lingered on the stage for a few minutes as the chants roared strong. He bent down to shake hands with admiring volunteers.

He stood upright and peered to the back of the room. Evana Bahar stood against the wall and signaled for him to come to her.

Fazil took his time before climbing down and weaving his way through the crowd. He shoved his hands in his pockets and sauntered up to her.

"Don't ever summons me like that again," Fazil said.

"Put your ego away, *cousin*," Evana said. "We have

far more pressing problems."

"What did you do this time?"

"I had a couple of people stop by my office today, claiming to work for *The Washington Post*. They asked me a bunch of questions about refugees and said they were working on an article about the plight of refugees worldwide."

"Who were they really?"

She shrugged. "I'm not sure, but their profile page doesn't look real. And no editor at the paper could confirm they actually worked for them, even in a freelance capacity."

"Who were they? MI5? MI6? CIA?"

"I'm not sure. I'll send you a picture from our security footage. All I know is that they came by my office and seemed pretty determined to get at me."

"You think they suspect you in some crime?"

"Probably not yet or else they would've already detained me."

Fazil sighed. "Is there something you want me to do about this?"

She shook her head. "I already took care of it."

"Did they give you anything?"

"A business card."

"And you took it?" Fazil asked, his eyes widening. "It could have had a tracker on it if they weren't who they said they were."

"I told you I handled it."

Evana crossed her arms and rapidly rubbed her skin in an attempt to warm herself.

Fazil looked her up and down. "What are you doing here without a jacket?"

"I'll tell you later. In the meantime, you can thank me for tripling the number of recruits you requested."

Fazil glared at her. "You think this is because of you? You insolent fool."

"You ask. I deliver. That's how this relationship works. And of course, you also pay me."

"Stop being so petty—and full of yourself. The reason why this building is teeming with young people itching to volunteer is because of the success we experienced a couple nights ago on London Bridge."

"You hijacked a drone only to lose it," she began as she counted off each point by grabbing one of her fingers. "You no longer have leverage because you returned a family you'd abducted. You didn't even kill a single infidel. I'm not sure how you think that's stirring up a resurgence of pride among Muslims, but you are Karif Fazil, the kid whose head was always too large for the biggest helmet I've ever seen."

Fazil smiled and shook his head. "That helmet was from a U.S. soldier. Also the first time I'd ever seen a dead body."

"You've seen plenty more since then—and you

might just see your own dying body if you're not careful."

Fazil glared at her. "We're going to have a long talk after this is over with about the way you speak to me."

CHAPTER 21

OUTSIDE A WAREHOUSE in Finsbury Park, two of Scotland Yard's finest CTC agents surveyed the activity. Hawk and Alex were watching the live feed on a series of monitors at Whitehall and listening in on the conversation between discussing their developments with Spiller and Admiral Riley.

"What's the connection to this building?" Spiller said.

Hawk took on the question. "Three months ago, it was leased by a shell corporation that we traced back to a Mediterranean bank that has handled scores of clients deemed terrorists in the past."

"That's enough to go on?" Spiller asked.

"That and the tracker I slipped into the collar of Evana Bahar's jacket is showing she's still there," Alex said.

"So you really think this ROARS director is connected to Al Hasib?" Riley asked.

"We're about to find out," Hawk said, nodding

toward the screens.

"What did she say to you when you questioned her?" Spiller asked.

Alex spun in her chair to face the two men. "We posed as journalists working with *The Washington Post* on a story about refugees."

"If she's the suspicious type, you know that she would try to verify your story," Spiller said.

"That's why we covered our tracks there," Alex said. "I set up dummy articles and fake LinkedIn profiles with our aliases. She would have to do a lot of digging to find out we weren't who we said we were."

"I wouldn't be so confident," Riley said. "Terrorists these days are more savvy than we give them credit for. They might hideout in caves and behave like savages, but they know how to operate secretly and securely in our digital age. We only catch them when they screw something up."

"Don't worry, Sgt. Spiller," Alex said. "This isn't our first rodeo."

"Yeah, but you don't typically do that type of reconnaissance work. Even the slightest thing could make her suspicious."

Hawk sighed. "Just relax, okay. The moment of truth is upon us. Those two CTC agents are simply waiting for the tactical team to join them. And according to their most recent transmission, the unit is just a few blocks away."

Hawk crossed his arms and stared at the screens, unwilling to even look at the two men holding an inquisition into Alex's actions. She put her hand on his shoulder and gave him a reassuring pat. The touch was quick but meaningful. He knew she appreciated his defense of her.

Two minutes later, the tactical team arrived and pulled up next to the agents' vehicle. They all piled out and suited up. Five minutes later, they surrounded the building and prepared to enter.

Hawk watched the screen as the two agents approached the door, accompanied by a dozen men decked out in armor of varying degrees and toting a shield and weapons.

"They look like they're ready for a shootout," Hawk said.

"That's not how we do things here," Riley said. "We talk first then shoot."

"Where's the fun in that?" Hawk said, trying to lighten the tense mood.

Riley didn't crack even the faintest smile. Neither did Spiller.

I'll never understand what makes Brits laugh.

Hawk diverted his attention to a couple screens that showed body cams from the tactical unit team members. The picture was a shaky one, but it presented a clear enough picture after a few seconds.

Sounds of "clear" resounded as the team members spanned out across the room and ventured into corridors and offices connected to the main space. The warehouse was almost completely empty.

"There's something in the center of the room," one of the men said. "I'm going to go check it out."

"Be careful," one of the MI5 agents said. "It could be a bomb."

Hawk watched the body cam feed that was now on the largest screen in the room. The tactical unit agent moved slowly toward what appeared to be a small table and a wooden chair with a jacket hung over the back. After a hesitant approach, the man picked up the jacket and inspected it. His eyes then fell on the table where there was a business card in the center. He picked it up and held it close enough so Hawk could read it.

Bianca Thurman, Washington Post

"Where is the tracking device?" Spiller asked.

"Underneath the collar," Hawk said.

"Check underneath the collar of the jacket," Spiller said over the coms to the agent.

He complied, and Hawk watched as a small device was retrieved from the spot where Alex had placed it.

"Looks like she was on to you," Spiller said.

Riley slammed his fist onto a desk and let out a string of expletives. "I told you not to be so confident. These people are good."

"At least we know to keep an eye on her now," Alex said. "She's got to be working with Fazil."

"She might be, but we just can't detain her because of a hunch," Riley said. "We need solid proof that she and Fazil are connected before we can go after her."

"I'll be happy to tail her," Alex said.

"She's not going to do anything stupid now," Spiller said. "I doubt she makes contact with him again after this stunt."

A man hustled over to Riley and whispered in his ear.

"It may not matter now," Riley said. "Fazil just called in and wants to speak with you, Hawk."

CHAPTER 22

FAZIL STARED AT THE PHOTO Evana had sent to his phone. He enlarged the image just to ensure he wasn't imagining things. He wasn't. The identities of the two mystery reporters who stopped by Evana's office were undoubtedly Brady Hawk and Alex Duncan.

Evana's text had also included the number on their business card. Fazil dialed it and waited for someone to answer. After a few rings, he hung up.

"Are you sure no one will be able to trace this phone?" Fazil asked.

The hacker known as Black Wolf sat at a desk in the corner of the room and shook his head.

"As long as you don't talk any longer than five minutes, they'll never track you down."

Fazil narrowed his eyes. "You better not be lying to me. If British government agents storm our offices, I'm shooting you first."

Black Wolf shrugged. "That's just as well. I'd rather not rot in a prison anyway."

Fazil returned his attention to the image.

You think you can just meddle in my business all the time. I'm going to take you out once and for all.

A couple minutes later, Fazil's phone rang with a number he didn't recognize.

"Can you tell me who this is?" Fazil asked.

Black Wolf stared at his screen, which tried to extrapolate the location of the number.

"I'm not sure," he said. "If you answer it, keep them on the line as long as possible, and I might be able to figure out where they are calling from."

Fazil accepted the call. "Yes."

"Karif Fazil," Brady Hawk said. "I was hoping to hear your voice. It's been a while."

"You're going to be disappointed in the outcome this time. I would advise you to leave London so you might live to fight another day."

"For all I know, today is all I have."

"Perhaps you're right, but if that's the case, it will be because of your own foolishness. I would advise you to stay out of this. I'll deal with you some other time. This attack is about settling a long-outstanding account."

"I know why you're here," Hawk said. "The sudden shift in the focus of your attack caught me off guard at first, but I know what you're doing. You're trying to get revenge on Davenport for giving the order to launch the drone attack that killed your father and brother."

Fazil looked at Black Wolf who held up both hands, signaling that he had ten seconds remaining.

"Well done," Fazil said. "Now that you've figured out my motive, good luck figuring out how to stop my next move. You're going to need it."

Fazil hung up the phone and shot a glance at Black Wolf. "Did we get his location?"

"The number was rerouted through a series of internet portals and switched several times by—"

"A yes or no answer will suffice," Fazil interrupted.

"Yes," Black Wolf said. "He's at the Ministry of Defense Whitehall building."

Fazil broke into a rage at the realization that Hawk was working with the British. Despite all Fazil's planning, he never anticipated that Hawk would come onto the scene. This was a personal matter between Fazil and Davenport, yet Hawk was apparently going to do what he did best—meddle with Fazil's plans.

"Can you track that phone?" Fazil asked.

"Only when it's turned on and the battery is inside," Black Wolf said. "And the battery was just removed."

"They must know you're working with me."

"That or they think that you have an advanced

tech team at your disposal. I'm supposed to be dead, remember?"

Fazil frowned. "But you're one of only a handful of people on the planet who can steal a drone. If they don't have your body somewhere, it would be dangerous to assume that they aren't going to come looking for you after something like this."

"I didn't really have a choice, did I?"

Fazil shrugged. "We always have a choice." He didn't believe a word of what he just said. If he told someone to do something, they better do it or else he would get rid of them. Technically, they still had a choice: comply or die.

Khetran entered the room and received a quick update from Fazil over the developments of the past quarter hour. During Fazil's relay of the information, Khetran opened his mouth to cut off Fazil several times but was brow beat into submission.

"Is there something you want to tell me?" Fazil finally asked after he was finished.

"There is, and I'm afraid it isn't good news."

Fazil took a deep breath and exhaled slowly. "Out with it."

"It's Davenport. He's gone missing."

CHAPTER 23

DAVENPORT SQUEEZED HIS EYES shut and tried to regain his wits. The lack of sleep had made everything hazy. He'd managed to stay coherent enough to kill the lone guard but just barely. That step was merely the first one—and likely the easiest. Escaping from a building presumably with heavily armed guards would present a more formidable challenge, especially since he had only a handful of shots with the guard's handgun.

Davenport leaned against a wall and took a deep breath. His attempted escape may have not been the most well-thought out thing he'd ever done, but survival instincts required that he fight. He presumed that at least his children were still alive, and they needed their father.

After settling his nerves, he began his escape attempt in earnest. He eased down a long corridor lit by alternating fluorescent bulbs overhead, before reaching an intersection. He decided to go left and noticed a plethora of hallways on both sides as he continued on. Cautiously, he peeked down each one before scurrying across. He wondered why the building was so quiet, especially if this was the central planning point for the attack. Even more puzzling to Davenport was his exact location. London had its share of vacant office buildings that had been rundown over time, yet usually not ones this large. This one seemed expansive—and, based on the décor, appeared to have been empty for a couple decades.

Where am I?

Davenport was sure he could figure it out, given enough time. He probably would've been able to recall the location off the top of his head had he not been so sleep deprived.

The sound of footsteps behind him jolted him back to the present. He darted down a corridor and scrambled to hide behind a desk sitting outside one of the offices. He wormed his way beneath the desk and lay prone, waiting for the guards to pass. He watched four sets of feet trample past, none even turning in his direction. Not that they would have reason to. The shadows and the furniture provided a sufficient cover from such a small search party.

After he was satisfied the guards were out of earshot, Davenport rolled out from beneath the desk and jumped to his feet. He decided to try one of the office doors. The first one he tried was locked. He stole down to the next door and turned the knob, which opened right up. Davenport eased inside, closing the door behind him. He rushed over to the window, which didn't have any blinds in it. Light from a street lamp shone inside, barely illuminating the room. There were still filing cabinets and a desk with a small couch and a couple of chairs.

Must've been an executive's office.

He poked his head around the corner of the windowsill to see if he could get a bearing on where he was and how easy it would be to get out. After a few moments of studying the grounds below, he was disappointed in his findings. He still had no idea where he was, nor did he think he'd be able to easily escape. A ten-foot high barbed-wire fence lined the side of the building, and he had no reason to believe it was any different anywhere else on the property.

He noticed an armed guard patrolling the area some fifty feet below. He was on what he surmised was the fifth floor of the complex. In order to escape, he needed not only to scale a tall fence—or cut his way through it—without getting seen. But only after he descended five flights of stairs and fought his way past a guard or two or six. The second Davenport discharged his weapon, his location would be inundated with Al Hasib agents trying to wrangle him.

Davenport held on to the shred of hope that Fazil still wanted him alive. And if that was the case, there wouldn't be a shoot-to-kill order out for Davenport. That was all he needed to have a fighting chance.

But it wouldn't be much of one if he couldn't figure out a way through. He glanced around the room, as if searching would help him give him the schematics of the facility. With the way his brain was working, he realized he needed some sleep, something he hadn't had in nearly forty-eight hours. But he couldn't just fall asleep on the floor. The Al Hasib guards would surely find him if they did a thorough sweep of the building.

Davenport glanced upward at the ceiling tiles. He jumped up on a desk and pried one of the rectangles loose. Dust flitted toward the ground. He swept the particles to the floor and hoisted himself up. The area above the room that remained hidden by the tiles was an entangled network of wires and tubing and piping. Davenport couldn't see any rhyme or reason to it, though he could follow the air duct. He put pressure on the duct, but it didn't move. He decided to hang from it and see how steady it was and if it would hold his weight. With metal support beams bolted to the wall and ceiling, the duct was virtually unmovable.

Perfect.

Davenport climbed all the way up onto the air

duct before carefully replacing the tile. He scooted into a prone position, allowing only his arms to hang off the sides. After a few minutes, he drifted off to sleep.

* * *

DAVENPORT AWOKE to a sharp poke in his ribs. A pair of cold rifle barrels nudged him a few times before he regained his bearings. He wasn't sure how long he'd been out—a minute? An hour? A day? Exhaustion had taken over, though based on the way he felt, he doubted he could've been out long. He still needed a cup of tea to wake up.

Davenport didn't get the chance to fully wake up before two large hands grabbed him, one near his shoulder and the other near his knee. With a quick yank, Davenport tumbled off the duct and through the ceiling, crashing hard to the floor. He missed smacking his head on the ground thanks to his hands cushioning the fall.

"Get up now," one of the men barked.

Davenport staggered to his feet. His slow movement only angered the guard more. He pulled his foot back and shoved it right into Davenport's backside. The momentum from the kick sent Davenport flailing forward toward the ground. He groped onto anything he could to retain his balance, grasping at one of the soldiers' pants. The fabric slid through Daveport's hands as he dropped back down to the floor, hitting it with a solid smack.

The guard yanked Davenport to his feet and signaled for two others to bind him up. They slapped a pair of handcuffs on him, ratcheting them as tight as they would go. The cold metal dug into Davenport's wrists.

"If Fazil didn't want you alive, I would finish you off myself right here," the guard whispered with a growl in Davenport's ear. "It's your lucky day, so to speak. You can best believe you're going to get a beating you'll never forget after killing one of my friends."

Davenport kept his eyes down, refusing to look at the guard. It wasn't a punch, but it was about the only way Davenport could fight back with his hands behind his back. Disrespect was a powerful weapon, the only one he could wield at the moment.

The guard grabbed Davenport's face. "Look at me when I'm talking to you. You're going to pay dearly for this."

Davenport diverted his eyes. The guard punched Davenport and then shoved him.

"Let's get you back to your cell where you belong."

The guard dialed a number on his phone and delivered the news.

"We caught him," he said. "He's still very much alive."

CHAPTER 24

HAWK LOOKED AT THE CLOCK as he entered Whitehall with a couple coffee cups. He handed them to the security guard, who made Hawk empty all his pockets before entering the metal detector. He looked back at Alex, who was following the same procedure.

"You're clear," the guard said, handing Hawk his drinks back.

Alex slid her cup around the edge of the scanner to another waiting guard.

"You Yanks need to learn how to drink tea," the guard snipped.

"I'm still trying to wake up," Alex said. "It's three o'clock in the morning where I live right now."

"Tea has caffeine in it, don't you know?" the guard fired back.

"But no triple shots of espresso," Alex said with a smile as she held up her cup.

"Have a nice day," the guard muttered as he gestured for her to continue.

Sgt. Spiller eased up beside them. "Seems like even our security guards here are on edge after all that's gone on this past week. Not everyone is so cross in the morning. And I'll let you in on a little secret."

"What's that?" Alex asked.

He glanced around and then spoke in a voice barely above a whisper. "There are quite a few Brits who like coffee, too."

Alex and Hawk chuckled and continued on to the command center.

"You might want to add a little extra coffee to your diet today," Spiller added. "I have a feeling it's going to be a long one."

"Anything that's happened overnight to make you believe that?" Hawk asked.

"Still no word from Fazil, and we have no idea if Davenport is alive or dead. Then there's the matter of Evana Bahar."

"That's what we want to tackle first," Hawk said.

Spiller swiped his access card in front of the security panel, and the doors unlocked. He tugged on the handle and allowed Alex and Hawk to enter the room first.

"Right this way," Spiller said, motioning for them to follow.

He led them to a small conference room, where Admiral Riley and other military brass were already waiting, seated around a large oval table. None of the men looked particularly happy, but Riley wore more furrowed lines in his brow than anyone else. His cheeks drooped along with large bags beneath his sunken eyes. His wispy gray hair appeared as though he hadn't even attempted to comb it.

"Any more developments you care to tell us about with regards to Evana Bahar?" Riley asked, dispensing with the formalities.

"I brought you some tea," Hawk said, placing the drink in front of Riley before taking a seat.

Riley held the cup up to his nose and inhaled a whiff before setting it back down. "Black tea," he said. "My favorite."

"I thought you might could use something to jumpstart your morning," Hawk said.

Riley took a sip before turning his focus back toward Hawk and Alex, who sat at the opposite end of the table from the British admiral.

"As I was saying," Riley continued, "are there any new developments after last night's embarrassing debacle?"

"I wouldn't call it embarrassing," Hawk said. "At least we know where Evana stands—and where her loyalties lie. It's all out in the open right now."

"Meanwhile, she's gone to ground," Spiller said, studying the dossier in front of him. "Apparently, local authorities along with MI5 agents have been unable to find her. And it might be a while before we see her again since we froze all her assets last night."

"I'm sure she has some stashed away for a rainy day," Hawk said. "She's no fool, especially if she's working with Fazil."

Spiller shook his head. "We all know that, but that's not something we can prove in court, at least not based on the information we have now. Leaving a jacket in an empty warehouse owned by a shell company in the Mediterranean is suspicious, but it won't hold up in our judicial system. Things are different than perhaps you're used to back home."

Alex crossed her arms. "We do take a little more leeway from time to time, but we still have plenty of burden of proof to deal with."

"Give us time," Hawk said. "We ought to be able to build a case against her. Let us work with some MI5 agents, and we'll see what we can do."

"There isn't time for that now," Spiller said. "We have more pressing matters."

"Such as?" Hawk asked.

"Fazil contacted us last night again after you went home," Spiller said. "Apparently, he forgot a few things and wanted to make sure we knew about them."

"What kind of grand prediction did he make?" Hawk asked.

"It wasn't a prediction," Riley said. "It was more like a 'save-the-date' notification."

"For when?" Alex asked.

"Tonight. Tower Bridge around midnight. He said we better be watching and warned us not to do anything stupid or else we would regret it," Riley said.

"Any idea what he's up to?" Hawk asked.

"Maybe a repeat performance of what he did with Davenport's family the other night," Spiller said.

"Doubt it," Hawk said. "If he does anything, he'll improve up on it—and I doubt he'll leave anything to chance."

"Well, we best get ready," Riley said. "I'm going to need more than one cup of black tea to help me see this thing through tonight with a clear mind."

"You and me both," Hawk said.

CHAPTER 25

FAZIL STOOPED OVER the shoulder of one of his assistants and dictated everything he wanted to share in the social media post. Convinced that the plan was failsafe, Fazil wanted the world to know about the show he was going to give them. And he couldn't wait.

"Are you sure you want to broadcast where this will take place?" the assistant asked. "Don't you want to have a bit of mystery?"

Fazil emphatically shook his head. "I want every single one of those infidels to know exactly where we'll be and how they can watch the destruction of one of the cities responsible for so much oppression of my brethren in the Middle East. It's a history they dare to be proud of. But I'll make them not only be ashamed but also regret that they ever started a fight with us."

The assistant nodded and continued typing.

Khetran entered the room and scanned the words on the screen still being massaged by Fazil.

"What do you think?" Fazil asked as he pounded his chest with his fist.

Jafar cooed and fluttered up to Fazil's shoulder.

Khetran arched an eyebrow. "It certainly lets everyone know that we're coming and where we'll be."

"Precisely what I want," Fazil said. "I want them to know I'm coming for them."

"I'm not convinced that's the best thing. If you give them time to prepare, they—"

"Eight hours to get ready for an onslaught that will rock their city worse than when the Germans bombed it? They'll have no idea how to stop what we're about to do, especially since we have a strategy that is sure to distract them. We tell them to look at my left hand while my right is poised to crash into their jaw."

"There is some merit behind this type of plan," Khetran said. "It's also fraught with danger. If they manage to sniff it out beforehand, everything could be in jeopardy."

Fazil shrugged. "Maybe, but no matter what happens in the end, all I know is that Liam Davenport will finally be held accountable for what he did to my family, especially my little brother. The entire world will know what he did and how the relentless assault on our people must stop or the westerners will suffer the consequences."

Khetran took a seat at the table across the room. "Do whatever you believe is best as it pertains to furthering our chances of making tonight a success and growing the ranks of Al Hasib. The more fighters we have, the better chance we have of taking the fight to these monsters and winning. But please don't let this be about your ego and your undying thirst for revenge. Such pursuits never end well for anyone."

"That is sound advice, just not for me in this situation," Fazil said. "I am going to make Davenport pay along with the rest of the warmongers who operate the government in this place overrun with infidels."

"I merely offer my suggestions," Khetran said. "In the grand scheme of things, you are the master of this realm. I will defer to you every time."

"As you should," Fazil said. "Now, let's go visit Mr. Davenport. I'm sure he's dying to see me again."

Fazil broke into a sly grin as he spun toward the door and gestured for Khetran to join.

* * *

FAZIL STEPPED ACROSS the threshold of the temporary holding cell created especially for Davenport. The British Secretary of Defense looked like he'd grown weary of defending anything. His tired eyes barely flickered when he looked at Fazil, a sign that the torture technique was working.

Fazil grabbed Davenport's chin and pushed it up, forcing his head back.

"I should just slit your throat right here for that stunt you pulled earlier," Fazil said. "After all, you can't claim to be insulated this time from any of the killing. You murdered my guard all on your own."

Davenport didn't flinch, much less respond.

"I remember the silent treatment," Fazil said. "One of my girlfriends from college refused to speak to me one night after she claimed I was a little too forceful with her. So I made her defiance more permanent by using duct tape on her mouth, which she couldn't get off for hours. That was the last time she ever treated me like that. There are always consequences—always."

Davenport's expression didn't change, unfazed by the threat.

"Perhaps I should put duct tape around your mouth and see how you like it. I'm not taking anything off the table since you need to be punished for your sins."

Davenport finally broke his silence. "If you're going to kill me, do it now. I'm tired of listening to you drone on with your endless drivel."

The inflammatory comment set off Fazil. He punched Davenport twice, once in the stomach and once more on the jaw. The second hit resulted in Davenport's head snapping back from the force of the blow. He went out cold as his head hung.

"You worthless infidel, tonight you will experience the full repercussions of your actions—both years ago and last night. No one gets away with murdering one of my men in cold blood. Or even my women for that matter. Such atrocities will not be ignored."

Fazil paced around the cell and awaited Davenport to awaken from the knockout punch. He regained consciousness groggily, still in a haze about what had just happened.

Fazil grabbed a cup of cold water from one of the other guards and splashed it on Davenport's face. The infidel's eyes widened.

"Mr. Davenport, you will regret the day you ordered the drone strike at a family wedding," Fazil began. "Your once proud city will be left in shambles after I decimate it with the help of some of my friends."

Davenport shook his head. "Your bravado is to be applauded, but you will rue the day you ever decided to pursue your revenge in this manner. You will be hunted down like a dog, your body splayed out on a London street somewhere without ever having realized your dream or attaining your revenge. Revenge is a empty mistress who will leave you cold and unsatisfied, never able to fully give you what you want and need."

"You speak boldly for a man who will soon be marched to his death," Fazil said. "Mr. Davenport, there's no one more dangerous than a man who has nothing to live for. Your people will learn a costly lesson tonight. You can't create monsters in the dark and expect them never to emerge in the light. When the world sees what you've done, they will reflect fondly on your very public demise. Tonight, I will be the one putting you down for good."

Davenport broke into a chuckle.

"Is something funny, Mr. Davenport?" Fazil asked.

"You still think you have a chance to do something," Davenport said. "You are delusional."

Fazil drew back his fist and drilled Davenport in the face. Davenport fell limp, his head slumping downward.

"I not only have a chance, but I have a foolproof plan. And you're going to pay the ultimate price," Fazil said, patting Davenport's cheek gently.

CHAPTER 26

HAWK AND ALEX SETTLED into their seats at the Ministry of Defense's command center at White-hall to get a final briefing as they ate a takeout dinner. Alex had spent most of the day chasing down more leads online pertaining to Evana Bahar. She hadn't reported into her office at ROARS and had only left a message on the general mailbox alerting the staff that she would be taking some personal time off. With Evana in the wind, Hawk used his time looking over schematics and working through potential scenarios with MI5 agents. As the day wound down, it appeared to be rather fruitless.

Hawk had just taken a bite of his fish when one of the agents tapped him on the shoulder.

"Mr. Hawk, there's someone on the line who wants to speak with you," he said.

Hawk finished chewing and washed down his food with a swig of water. "Who is calling for me?"

"We believe it's Karif Fazil."

Hawk glanced at Alex. "Here we go."

"Try to keep him on the line as long as possible," the agent said. "I'm sure you know the drill."

Hawk nodded and took the receiver, raising it to his ear. "This is Hawk."

"I was hoping you would be there," Fazil said. "But let's be honest, I already knew you were going to be there. In fact, I have eyes on you at all times."

"If you're going to be honest, at least be honest about it. I know you can't see me now."

Fazil clucked his tongue. "Don't be so sure. Al Hasib's network is far reaching. We have our tentacles in places that even you would be shocked to hear."

"Like in the British Ministry of Defense?"

"Exactly. Better be careful. I could give the word, and one of my agents in the room would shoot you in the head before you could figure out what day of the week it is."

"I'm not interested in playing your mind games tonight," Hawk said.

"Then maybe you'd like to play something else."

"Since we're on this new honesty kick, I'm not really in the mood for games of any kind right now."

"That's disappointing because I have one that I think you would enjoy. It's called rescue the secretary of defense."

"Sounds rather unimaginative, if you ask me."

"Why would you say that, Brady? You don't even know how it's played."

"I think I have a pretty good idea of how it goes."

Fazil laughed. "Perhaps, but I'd be surprised if you thought the game ended with you being successful. I'll let you in on a little secret: The game ends when London goes . . ." He paused for dramatic effect. "Boom!"

Hawk looked over at the technical team. He gestured as if to question if they had traced the call yet. One of the agents shook his head but motioned for Hawk to continue.

"Like I said, sounds rather unimaginative to me. No matter what you think, we've played this game before. And I always seem to win. I doubt this time will be any different."

"That's where you're wrong," Fazil said. "I admit that I have not been a worthy opponent recently. You've been able to foil some of my plots, sometimes due to the fact that I poorly designed the operation, other times thanks to your quick-witted thinking. But this time, I'm already one step ahead of you."

"What do you want?" Hawk asked as he glanced at the agents still trying to get a location. One of them shook his head and gestured for Hawk to keep trying.

"Isn't it obvious by now? You know exactly what I want."

"Revenge," Hawk said. "You want revenge. And you think that killing Davenport is going to give that to you."

"That's not all."

"I'm sure you have designs set on doing something else as well, but your main purpose is to avenge your family's death. We've been at this long enough. It's no secret."

"Then why ask?"

"You need to know that what you're doing will not end well for you. There is always a price to pay for revenge."

"Yes, yes. I've heard it all before. But this is about more than just revenge. This is jihad."

"I thought we were being honest with one another. We both know this has nothing to do with jihad."

"You infidels are all the same. You'll never understand."

"I'm afraid I understand all too well. You're not the first person to co-opt your religion as an excuse to crusade against others."

Fazil was silent for a moment before continuing. "Carry on with all your assumptions but know that they will come back to haunt you. You underestimate the determination of a devout man at your own peril."

"We'll see who's underestimating who real soon, won't we?"

"I'm sure you saw the update on Al Hasib's social

media channels," Fazil said. "I'll be ready for anything you might attempt. Midnight on the Tower Bridge. It will all be over with after that."

Hawk glanced at the technical staff where one of the members looked wide-eyed and motioned with his hand to keep going.

Fazil hung up.

A string of expletives flew from the tech staff.

"We almost had him," one of the men said. "We just needed you to keep him on the line for another fifteen seconds."

Hawk shook his head. "You think he didn't know that too? He's got to be working with Black Wolf. And that man rarely makes mistakes, if any."

"Are you ready to get back to work?" Spiller asked. "We have plenty of logistical issues to discuss before it gets too late."

"What exactly do you expect me to do tonight?" Hawk asked.

"We were hoping you might be able to save Davenport," Admiral Riley said.

"And how, exactly, do you expect me to do that? Fazil will have a way out of every situation. There won't be anything we do that he wouldn't have accounted for, including someone crashing his party."

"Then let's do something he wouldn't expect, even from you," Riley said.

Blunt lumbered up to the table and fell into a seat next to Hawk. "If anyone can throw Fazil off his game, it's Hawk."

"I might be able to save Davenport, but that doesn't mean I'll be able to stop the attacks Fazil has planned for tonight on London," Hawk said. "We don't even know what he's planning on targeting yet."

Alex hammered away on her keyboard before stopping abruptly. "I think I might know what he's up to, but we need to act fast. This city might be in ashes if we don't move quickly."

CHAPTER 27

DAVENPORT STOPPED TO FEEL the breeze whipping down the Thames. He wasn't sure if he'd ever get another chance and wanted to soak in the last moments of his life. The sharp jab to his back snapped Davenport out of his fantasy that he was alone. He reacted to the poke, bending backward before stumbling forward. In an instant, the pleasant sensation of wind on his face was replaced with the searing pain in his chest and back from the beating he had taken earlier that evening. The handcuffs dug into his wrists, creating another uncomfortable feeling.

He marched forward per Fazil's instructions. Slow and steady steps kept Davenport upright as he moved, otherwise he would've toppled over. He felt weak, his strength gone due to sleepless nights and malnourishment. The fact that his body could deteriorate so rapidly boggled his mind. But he doubted he helped. Since the moment he discovered his family had been taken, Davenport could feel the ulcer in his stomach eating away at him. He couldn't stop being anxious, not even for a second. When Evelyn was still alive, he worried if she could make it and how she was handling the kids. As he walked toward his death, his thoughts were consumed with his children.

Is this how they'll remember me?

The thought was equally sobering and terrifying. High atop the Tower Bridge, Davenport couldn't change much of anything. He itched his sides and adjusted the suicide vest, the one Fazil attached just a half hour ago. Davenport wondered if he would blow apart and take the bridge down with him. Would his name become synonymous with the London landmark, forever reminding his children of their father's inability to protect them?

All because I wanted one last hug.

They didn't know the truth, but he did. And he couldn't shake free the idea the whole ordeal was indeed his fault. No matter how crazy Karif Fazil was, ultimately Davenport's decision to bomb that family wedding had far-reaching repercussions. At the time, it was just another head nod, another rubber stamp on a request from one of his trusted advisors. And despite the consequences, Davenport wasn't sure he'd do anything differently. Maybe there was one thing.

I'd send them straight to the country and visit them later.

Davenport tried to stay focused for his children's

sake. He wanted to fight but couldn't. He wanted to jump but realized that would be a leap to almost certain death. He wanted to close his eyes and wake up from a horrible nightmare with Evenlyn next to him in the bed. But fate had dealt him a different hand, one he could only win with a bluff.

His eyes lit up with the thought.

Maybe I could steal Fazil's thunder and force him to fold.

The idea was a long shot, but it was worth a try. Every other option Davenport considered seemed destined to fail. Yet it would only work if Fazil's motives were as Davenport assumed. But did he know the Al Hasib leader enough to ascertain such information?

If Fazil's end game was simply to kill Davenport and do it in the most public way possible, it wouldn't matter what he did. At the end of this ordeal, death was inevitable. But what if it wasn't. What if there was something else Fazil wanted, something he desired more than revenge. Could Davenport give it to him?

"Why are you doing this?" Davenport said, beginning his probe.

Fazil sighed. "We've been over this before. Do I really need to spell it out for you?"

"You and I both know there's more to this than revenge, right? Jihad? Power? A legacy? What is it that drives you to take action like this? Is that how you want the world to remember you?"

Fazil wouldn't participate in Davenport's game, instead shoving him forward down the walkway with a gun planted firmly in his back.

"You're starting to annoy me," Fazil finally said.

Davenport took a deep breath and pondered his next question. Before he had a chance to ask it, Fazil pointed toward the top of the tower.

Davenport stopped and glanced down at the water below. They were a hundred and eighty feet above the waters that sloshed along thanks to the windy conditions. He looked up at the tower and then back toward Fazil.

"What do you want me to do?" Davenport asked.

"We're going up," Fazil said. "I want to be as high as possible for all of this."

"But how?" Davenport asked. "There aren't any stairs."

Fazil unlocked Davenport's handcuffs and hitched himself to his prisoner with a rope. When finished, Fazil pointed again toward the top of the turret closest to the east bank.

"We're going to climb."

CHAPTER 28

HAWK STOLE A GLANCE at Blunt, who had gnawed the end of his cigar flat. He was the only one who gave off the semblance of being calm, though Hawk knew better. Blunt never ground his stogie into nothing unless he was nervous. The rest of the people working in the command center at Whitehall didn't attempt to hide their panic.

The bank of screens on the back wall showed every available CCTV in the area of the Tower Bridge. Hawk noticed the Union Jack whip furiously atop the structure as Davenport and Fazil worked their way up the turret. A climbing rope kept the two men tethered, while Fazil had anchored himself to the railing on the walkway, ensuring Davenport couldn't make a surprise jump that would kill them both.

One of the tactical team leaders approached Admiral Riley, who was running the operation.

"I think we should take a head shot," the leader said. "I have word from several of my snipers that we could eliminate the hostile."

Riley arched an eyebrow and looked up at the screens. "Even in this wind?"

"They're the best we have, and I trust them."

Riley shook his head. "Not yet. We still have plenty to sort out before we can start firing at will on Fazil. At this point, we need a better idea of what he plans to do."

"When will we know that?"

"One of our analyst friends from the U.S. is working on that as we speak," Riley said before dismissing the man.

Hawk eased over to Alex, whose gaze was locked in on the computer screen in front of her. He gave her a gentle, reassuring rub on her back and settled into the seat next to her.

"Don't you have the world to go save?" she snapped.

"Sorry, I wasn't trying to bother you," Hawk said. "I just wanted to see how you were doing and how things were going."

"You know my sarcasm comes out strongest in the heat of battle," she said. "Now, I'd appreciate it if you would leave me alone and let me see if I can extrapolate what all this means."

Hawk stood and backed away. A few minutes earlier, Alex had made a discovery on Evana Bahar's computer, an action Alex took on her own without the knowledge of the British government officials. She figured if what she found helped stop London being turned into a pile of rubble, nobody would mind.

She had been going through Evana's file all afternoon and couldn't find a single thing that looked suspicious. Alex used encryption programs to search for locked files that might be hiding the information about the attacks. But nothing.

That's when Alex glanced at the screensaver carousel of images. At first, they seemed like just another collection of photos of London. But Alex opened one of them up and noticed some garbled messages embedded into the metadata. She dropped a few phrases into one of her code-breaking algorithms and cracked it a few minutes later. The pictures were far more than just a screensaver—they were the targets. Stuffed into the metadata of each photo were dimensions of the landmark or building along with how much explosives were estimated to bring it down. Just to be sure she wasn't imagining everything, Alex took the time and date stamped on the photo and cross-referenced it with CCTV footage to see if she could identify who took each picture. Knowing the perspective of the image helped speed the process along.

The photographers were a number of different

people, including Evana at two different sites: Big Ben and London Tower. Alex isolated the people who appeared to be taking the pictures and ran them through facial recognition software. She was waiting for the results to hand off to London authorities to start hauling the men in for questioning. However, she wondered if it would be too little too late.

"I've got the names," she said triumphantly as she held up a piece of paper.

One of the taskforce team members rushed over to get it from her and then scurried away.

"Good work," Riley said.

"My work is far from over," she said. "We've got forty-five minutes before Fazil's promised show begins."

Hawk sauntered back over to the television screens. He was joined by several aides who scanned the images on the wall.

"What is he doing?" one of the men asked.

"He's getting the audience he wants," Hawk said.

"Think he'd be willing to trade Davenport for something?"

Hawk shot the man a sideways glance. "Fazil already made his trade and got exactly what he wanted, thanks to Davenport's reckless move. This isn't about a negotiation. This is about to be a demonstration. Al Hasib glory footage in real time."

"We can't just let him die," one of the men said.

"He's right," Riley said as he butted into the conversation. "We can't let Davenport die like this. It'd be too humiliating for us as a country."

Hawk sighed. "Well, what do you want to do? Take a head shot? Risk Davenport dying from a fall anyway, not to mention all the bombs that might go off simultaneously if Fazil is dead."

"We're securing all the buildings and landmarks Al Hasib was planning on targeting even as we speak," Riley said.

Hawk watched Blunt lumber across the room, this time with a fresh cigar to chew.

"Are we going to stand around here with ours heads up our asses, or are we gonna take down that piss ant?" Blunt asked.

"I was hoping you had some suggestions," Riley said. "We're running out of time."

Hawk took a deep breath and studied the picture, focusing on Fazil and Davenport atop the Tower Bridge.

"Okay," Hawk said. "I've got an idea."

"What kind of idea?" Riley asked.

"We're just sitting here, letting Fazil dictate everything at his own leisure. Who cares about his midnight deadline. Let's put the pressure on him, make him move it up or switch things, force him into a

212 | R.J. PATTERSON

mistake. Our passive approach right now is kind of like letting Ronaldo and Real Madrid work over your favorite premier league soccer team. What we need to do is put his head in a vice grip."

"That's a great halftime pep talk," Riley said, "but we need something more actionable than that."

"I know," Hawk said. "I'll explain more later, but there's something I need to know first."

"What's that?" Riley asked.

"Does anyone know where I can get a parachute suitable for base jumping?"

CHAPTER 29

A QUARTER HOUR BEFORE midnight, Davenport felt his hands begin to slip against the stone at the top of the Tower Bridge. His feet were secure, but his palms were dripping sweat. The flag snapped back and forth, cracked by the force of the wind. A light drizzle pelted him in the face. This wasn't how he envisioned his life ending, not even when he was stuck in a cell just a few hours ago.

He glanced at his watch. Each second that ticked past seemed to disappear at a painfully slow rate. Had the situation been any different, he would've preferred to have the end of his life slow down. But all he wanted was for the mind games to end. He'd already resigned himself to the fact that Fazil was going to kill him—and do it in dramatic fashion. A bullet to the back of the head and a long tumble into the Thames, joining all the other embedded agents who'd been outed by Fazil a week before. That seemed like the way Fazil was going to play this. But Davenport couldn't be sure of anything.

Craning his neck to see the water just below the bridge, he leaned forward. His feet slipped for the first time since he'd been forced to climb up by Fazil. Davenport could feel a knot forming in his calves, undoubtedly from staying in the same position on his haunches for over a half hour and remaining so tense. A searing pain began to spread up his back. He grimaced and moaned.

Fazil broke into a chuckle. "Hurts like hell, doesn't it?"

Davenport didn't move, much less acknowledge the comment.

"I've been in your situation before," Fazil said. "There's a point when you must press through the pain because of the reward that lies beyond."

Davenport took a deep breath and exhaled, refusing to engage Fazil any more.

"You think you're tough, maybe even clever," Fazil continued. "But in the end, you are a failure, just like all those agents who were found floating along this very river. You gave your life to protect this country, but what has it amounted to? It has cost you everything. Your family, your wife, and, very soon, your own life. You have to ask yourself: Was it worth it? In a moment like this, right before you die, you don't think about that. You try to dwell on the positive, the things you enjoyed in your time on earth. And you better because you are an infidel, and you're about to experience pain beyond all you could ever imagine as the flames of Hell will lap at you for eternity."

"Your day will come too," Davenport finally said, breaking his vow to stay quiet. "It may come sooner than you think. I suppose you're having these thoughts as well right now."

Fazil laughed. "Oh, my dear Mr. Davenport, you have such a sense of humor, even in a time like this."

"I've been in war enough to know that death and life—those moments when you truly come alive— occur when you least expect them. You can't plan for them. You can't schedule them. They just happen."

"You may be right, most of the time. But tonight, I have planned for this very night for a long time. And I can assure you that I will be fully alive as I watch London burn to the ground."

Fazil shifted his weight, giving a sharp tug on the rope that tethered him to Davenport.

"Stand up," Fazil said as he looked at his watch. "It's almost time."

Davenport complied and proceeded to tug sharply on the rope. Fazil didn't move.

He sneered at Davenport. "Don't worry. I will set you free very soon."

* * *

HAWK WAS RUSHED to the Tower Bridge via a police escort. He tugged on the straps to his parachute, pulling them taut. He checked his two guns once more. As much as he wanted Fazil dead, Hawk needed questions answered first. Even still, he wasn't sure he'd have enough time to get them before Al Hasib started raining down terror on London.

Hawk approached the bridge stealthily from the tower opposite Fazil and Davenport. Figuring a visible approach would be more conducive to talking than a surprise appearance, Hawk scampered up the stairs, reaching the bridge that connected the two turrets in less than a minute. He entered the bridge with both hands raised in the air.

"Fazil, we need to talk," Hawk said.

Fazil glanced down at the bridge and swung his gun around, training it on Hawk.

"Don't come any closer," Fazil said. "This doesn't concern you, Hawk. I will deal with you when I'm finished. Or I could just shoot you now."

"Maybe," Hawk said. "Or maybe you'd never see your brother again either."

"What are you talking about?" snarled Fazil. "I cradled my brother in my arms as he died. I buried him."

"That's a touching story, but one you know is a complete lie," Hawk said.

"That's not true," Fazil said, shaking his gun at Hawk. "Leave me alone. You spew nothing but lies, you infidel."

"If I'm telling lies, why not just shoot me?" Hawk said. "I'm not holding a weapon. I just want to get my friend back here."

"This is someone you call a friend? A man who gives the order to murder innocent children? While we might have different objectives, Mr. Hawk, I always thought you were a decent man. But not anymore."

"Then shoot me," Hawk said. "There are snipers all over. We know what you're planning on doing with the secretary of defense. And we know what you want to do to this city. Be careful because your next move could be fatal."

Fazil shook his head. "No matter what you think you know, you know nothing. You kill me, you will helplessly watch this city burn to the ground."

"Mr. Davenport didn't kill your brother," Hawk said. "He's still alive."

Fazil's eyes narrowed. "I saw it myself. I was there. He died after a missile from one of those Reaper drones annihilated the wedding. My father died too."

"Your father died, but he was a monster. But not your brother. I know where he is."

Fazil fired a warning shot that skipped off the

bridge a few feet from where Hawk was standing. The combination of the wind and the recoil jolted Fazil backward. He stutter stepped and then regained his balance.

Hawk shot a quick glance up at Davenport, who was fiddling with the rope tied around his waist. He appeared to subtly loosen the cord while covering it with his hand so Fazil couldn't see what was happening.

"This man is innocent of the very thing you're condemning him for," Hawk said. "The whole world is watching you right now. Do you think you will be able to rally much support after you're dead and they all know that your entire story was a lie?"

"This is about *jihad* too, make no mistake," Fazil said. "We are fighting against the evil forces of the west. It's not about one drone strike. It's been going on for far too long, and it must come to an end. Tonight, this city will pay for its transgressions, and this man will be judged accordingly."

"Let him go, Fazil," Hawk said. "If you do, I'll make arrangements for you to be reunited with your brother."

* * *

DAVENPORT FELT the blood leave his face. He struggled to swallow as his mouth went dry. Looking down at the water below, he wondered if he had a chance of surviving the drop from over two hundred feet.

With Brady Hawk attempting to entice Fazil with the possibility of seeing his brother, Davenport realized that the situation had reached a point where the decision makers in his absence had decided to make one final attempt. And from what Davenport knew, it was doomed from the start. Fazil's brother was dead and buried. He'd seen a picture of his body following the drone strike. This was strictly a mind game Hawk was playing, anything to throw Fazil off. His desire to see his brother alive again might make Fazil start to question his sanity. That had to be the objective, because Fazil wasn't about to let the opportunity to slip away from him.

Davenport held the loosened rope in his hands. All that was left was to ease into a better position so he could jump. He noticed the London police officers patrolling the Thames on jet skis.

If I survive, maybe they can drag me ashore.

Davenport had no idea what to expect if he hit the water at that speed from that height. He didn't know if it would knock him out or kill him instantly. He wished he had time to research the answer, but there was no opportunity to do that. All that was left to do was leap and pray.

He cut a quick glance toward Hawk, who was still

trying to persuade Fazil into releasing his hostage. But Fazil set his jaw and fought off every heart-tugging overture.

This isn't going anywhere.

Davenport studied the water for a moment more before gathering his nerve. He took a deep breath and dropped the rope, unfurling it from around him.

Then he jumped.

* * *

HAWK WONDERED HOW long he could hold Fazil at bay with the story about his brother still being alive. It wasn't likely to work, but Hawk had to try something.

The key to talking down a hostage taker is to make a human connection and remind them of their humanity, maybe even convince them they have something to live for, even if a long jail sentence is in their future. Give them long enough to think about it, and they might cave during a moment of weakness. That split second was all any negotiator could hope for.

But this scenario had a wrinkle to it: the hostage was considered a risk to jump.

As Hawk made preparations at Whitehall, the discussion centered around all the possible outcomes. Fazil could detonate Davenport's suicide vest, killing both of them and damaging the bridge. That was the worst case. They could shoot Fazil and have a chance of saving Davenport as long as they didn't both fall from atop the Tower Bridge and plunge into the water. The outcome there was reduced to a coin flip as to whether Davenport would survive. Then there was the possibility that Davenport could jump.

Hawk was convinced Davenport would take a risk, though nothing was a certainty. The defense secretary had already proven to have the kind of nerves necessary to take such an action. His attempt to exchange himself for his family might have indeed saved his children even if it was ill-advised.

The question Hawk had pondered as he climbed the steps a few moments before was if Davenport jumped, would Fazil explode the vest. And Hawk still wasn't sure what Fazil would do.

"Enough of your lies," Fazil roared. "I held my brother's dead body. Your time is almost up, Mr. Hawk, as is this city's. You made a foolish mistake in trying to get involved, and now you're going to die along with this pathetic excuse for a human being."

Hawk watched Davenport drop the rope and crouch down before leaping from the turret and out over the water. Sensing what was happening, Hawk already had one hand on the railing. He propelled himself over and right into a collision course with Davenport.

The two men collided hard, but Hawk had the

wherewithal to wrap his legs around Davenport and yank his parachute cord. The fall was fast and furious, and Hawk did everything in the small window of one second that he needed to do in order to have a chance.

The chute deployed with just enough wind filling it a half second before they would've hit the water. However, they still fell fast, hitting the water with a splash. Hawk released his harness and grabbed hold of Davenport's arm.

"Stay with me," Hawk said as he swam toward the shore.

A police officer on a jet ski rumbled up next to them and started asking them if they needed help. Hawk was distracted by the helicopter that was headed straight for the Tower Bridge. A long rope hung from the aircraft.

The chopper hovered above Fazil just long enough for him to grab the rope and secure himself. With a thumbs-up gesture, the helicopter resumed its flight over the Thames.

Hawk looked at the officer. "Yes, I do need your help. I need your jet ski."

"I'm sorry, sir, but I'm not authorized to—"

Hawk wasn't interested in hearing the rest of the officer's spiel. Fazil would be three sheets to the wind if Hawk didn't commence an immediate pursuit.

Using the side of the jet ski to hoist himself out

of the water, Hawk grabbed the officer and pulled him into the river. The move caught the officer by surprise as he fell headlong.

"Sorry," Hawk said as he sped away. "Help get your secretary of defense to shore, and then get him a towel."

Hawk gunned the motor and scanned the skyline for the chopper. It was nowhere to be seen.

CHAPTER 30

Ministry of Defense Whitehall

ALEX GASPED AS SHE watched the scene unfold on the bank of monitors in front of her. The frenetic pace even stirred Blunt to get up from his seat and stare wide-eyed at the screens. Although Alex had been silent during the tense moment atop the Tower Bridge, she let out a sigh of relief and went to work.

"Nice job," Alex said into her coms.

"I'm not done yet," Hawk answered over the whine of the jet ski's engine.

"No, you're not. Do you still have a visual on the target?"

"Negative. I'm just going in the direction I last saw the chopper."

"I've got him," Alex said. "They are heading west, staying over the river for some reason."

"That can't be good," Hawk said. "He's probably going to light up half of this city."

"The ministry of defense and MI5 are coordinating with local law enforcement," she said. "Everyone is out on patrol looking for any potential suicide bombers and combing for explosives at all the major buildings and landmarks that I uncovered on Evana's computer."

"Are you sure you were right about those sites?"

"I'm never certain about anything in these situations, but that's my best educated guess."

"Any idea how we can nail down the exact time and locations? Fazil promised a show at midnight, and the clock is about to strike twelve."

"He stopped streaming after Davenport jumped, but he was texting before the helicopter arrived."

"If I can get his phone, maybe I can get an exact location for these bastards."

"How do you plan to do that?"

"Tell the snipers to start firing on the chopper, but we need Fazil alive. Just keep watching."

Alex turned her attention back to the screen when the power went out.

* * *

HAWK TRIED TO TURN the throttle back, but it wouldn't budge. He was running wide open along the rough water and hoping he could get some help. As he came around the bend, the helicopter turned back into view with Fazil still dangling from the rope.

Hawk considered pulling his weapon out for a moment but decided against wasting any rounds. The snipers had more powerful bullets and a better chance of hitting the target than he did.

Seconds later, sparks started flying off the side of the aircraft. Six, seven, eight shots peppered the fuselage. A moment later, smoke streamed out of the chopper, sending it in a spiral toward the water near Westminster Bridge.

Hovering about thirty meters above the water, Fazil let go of the rope and fell feet first into the Thames. Hawk was still a half-mile away but could see everything unfolding. He navigated the jet ski toward the south side of the river where Fazil was now swimming furiously toward the bank.

Hawk closed the distance between them quickly. As he neared the bank, he watched Fazil scramble up the side and head for Westminster Bridge.

"Alex," Hawk said in his com. "Can you hear me?"

"I can, but I can't see a thing," she said. "The power just went out here. I'm flying blind."

"In that case, tell someone to get London officers to close off Westminster Bridge immediately. There's still traffic on it at this time of night, and people are going to be in danger. Fazil is desperate now."

Fazil raced along the sidewalk skirting the bridge, frantically scanning the area. With a gun in one hand and a phone in the other, he checked over his shoulder for Hawk.

Hawk drew his weapon and sprinted toward Fazil. While running toward the north side of the river, Fazil fired a couple shots in Hawk's direction. Both of them sailed past harmlessly.

Hawk looked up to see several vehicles moving toward them, including a double-decker bus. The motorists slowed down, likely taken aback by the gun-wielding men racing down the sidewalk. One of the cars had slowed down to no more than five miles an hour and had the bus on its tail as it approached Fazil. Without hesitating, Fazil fired a shot at the driver, killing him instantly and sending the car halfway up onto the curve before bouncing off the railing and back into the roadway.

The bus hadn't slowed down as much and didn't have as much time to react. Trying to compensate for the vehicle sitting sideways across two lanes of traffic, the bus driver jerked the wheel left and then right, getting the bus off balance. On the second quick turn, it fell onto its side and skidded across the pavement as sparks flew.

With a handful of cars still on the bridge heading toward them, Fazil rushed into the road and pointed his gun at one of the motorists. Gesturing for him to get out, Fazil opened the door and hurried the process along by snatching the driver by the collar and hurling him into the street. Then Fazil shot him in the head before climbing behind the wheel.

Hawk raced toward the wreckage, wondering if the chaos was created in hopes of distracting him from the mission. There were several bodies strewn across the bridge, but Hawk couldn't do much for them and continued on knowing that if Fazil escaped, hundreds if not thousands more people would die.

"Alex, send a slew of paramedics to Westminster Bridge," Hawk said. "There are injuries including an overturned bus."

"Roger that. Do you have eyes on Fazil?"

"He's driving away, but not for long."

Hawk took aim at the tires of the vehicle Fazil had just hijacked. After three shots, the back right tire blew out and spun the car around. The rest of the cars that had been on the bridge had had already turned in the opposite direction.

Fazil leapt out of the car and fired a shot at Hawk. Using the vehicle as cover, Fazil knelt behind it and ripped off another couple shots.

Hawk scrambled back behind the double decker, shielding himself from the onslaught of bullets. As Hawk counted the shots, he deduced Fazil had brought at least two clips and figured he had only about eight bullets left.

The two inoperable vehicles were about thirty meters apart as the two men dug into their positions.

"Time's up, Fazil," Hawk said. "You know this is over."

"For you maybe, but not for me," Fazil said. "Even if I die tonight, my legacy will live on. This city and this country will never forget my name."

"I wouldn't be so sure if I were you. You're going to be a footnote, nothing more."

"Guy Faulks failed and lived in infamy."

"You're no Guy Faulks."

"Are you sure about that?" Fazil asked with a chuckle.

"Alex," Hawk said into his com links. "Were the Houses of Parliament on that list of potential targets?"

"I don't recall seeing it on there," she said.

"Well, get someone over there now. Fazil just tipped his hand."

Fazil fired off a couple shots, keeping Hawk pinned down.

"What's the matter, Hawk? Afraid to come out and play?"

He's got six shots left.

Hawk peeked around the back corner of the bus

and saw Fazil standing upright. Hawk squeezed off three rounds, all missing just around Fazil.

"You're not shooting like someone who was trained in the Navy Seals," Fazil said, goading Hawk on. "My aunt could shoot a weapon better than that."

Hawk eased back out and fired off two more shots, both missing."

"One more shot, Hawk, then what are you going to do?" Fazil asked.

Hawk needed help in the worst way, but with Alex unable to assist, he was stuck trying to figure a how to escape the jam on his own.

"How does it feel to know that all this time tracking me down is going to be in vain?" Fazil continued, shooting a pair of rounds in Hawk's direction. "Is that the last thing you'll think about before you die?"

"Why don't I let you answer that question," Hawk said. "You're the one who has wasted your life trying to get revenge. And now you're finding it's an empty, hollow feeling."

"No, it feels good," Fazil said as he shot twice more at Hawk. "Watching Mr. Davenport as he listened to the explosion that killed his wife—it was all worth it."

"It doesn't change a thing for you and your family."

"Yes, it does. Justice was served."

"That wasn't justice," Hawk said before peering around the corner and firing another shot.

"Is that fuel spilling out of the back of that bus?" Fazil asked. "And just in time for you to run out of bullets."

Hawk inhaled, catching the scent of the gas that was spewing out of the bus and onto the bridge. He looked down to see it pooling around his feet.

"Goodbye, Brady Hawk," Fazil said before he fired two more shots, the second one sparking a fire that swarmed around the bus.

Hawk raced toward the other end, as far away from the tank as he could get. A fiery explosion ensued and engulfed the back end of the bus. It spread quickly toward the front. He knelt in front and shielded his face from the heat. He was almost certain that Fazil was out of ammunition.

Hawk contemplated retreating a safe distance from the bus before it completely exploded, but he figured that would give Fazil enough time to escape, maybe even disappearing again for a long time. And who knows what other places Al Hasib planned to attack tonight.

Hawk crept forward before dashing into plain view at the opposite end of the bus where he'd been.

Fazil stood upright and unguarded for a moment, as if he was admiring his work.

Hawk didn't hesitate. He pumped two shots into Fazil's chest, sending him sprawling backward. Hawk rushed over to his victim to see if he was still alive and to retrieve his phone.

Blood pooled around Fazil as he clutched his chest and gasped for air. His gun had tumbled a few feet away. Hawk slid the gun farther away with his foot and kept his weapon trained on Fazil.

"Does your aunt shoot like that?" Hawk asked.

Fazil smiled and shook his head. He struggled to speak between wheezing breaths.

"Your day will come very soon, Mr. Hawk."

"But it won't be today," Hawk said. "Goodbye, Fazil."

Hawk fired once more, hitting Fazil in the head and killing him instantly. It was a far more merciful death than he deserved, but Hawk didn't have time to watch his formidable foe bleed out.

Hawk's night had only just begun.

CHAPTER 31

HAWK FISHED FAZIL'S PHONE out of his
pocket and stared at the screen. To gain access, a password was required. A thumbprint would also work.
Hawk grabbed Fazil's lifeless hand and depressed his
thumb on the button. The phone opened right up.

"Alex," Hawk said. "Are you still available?"

"Power just came back on," she said. "There was
a problem with the emergency generation, but now
everything is rebooting. What's your status?"

"Fazil is dead," he said. "I'm scrolling through
his phone now."

"How did you—"

"He didn't object to me using his thumb," Hawk
said, anticipating her question. "Now, tell me what I'm
looking for."

"Search his texts and previous phone calls," she
said. "We think that's how he was communicating with
his cell."

"Can you trace some numbers for me?" he asked.

"Well, if you call them and someone answers, we can."

"I'll give you the numbers, and you can have someone there start tracing these. How does that sound?"

"Go for it."

Hawk rattled off four phone numbers as well as the number on his phone. He dialed each, waited for someone to pick up, and said nothing. He tried to keep them on the line for as long as possible before hanging up. He tried whispering something in Arabic, like he was hardly able to speak. It made the caller reticent to hang up.

Crouched next to Fazil's body, Hawk watched the emergency responders start hosing down the bus and putting out the fire before entering. One fireman motioned furiously to his colleagues for a stretcher. A minute later, a person was being carted toward an ambulance that had just arrived. Based on the fire, Hawk was surprised anyone was still alive. Most of the sparse riders who were able had escaped when the bus skidded to a stop, scrambling out of the windows. But apparently at least one person had survived the first. Hawk hated the fact that anyone else on board likely gave their life so Fazil could be stopped. It was a sacrifice the person didn't make, but one that would extend the lives of countless others.

"Anything yet?" Hawk asked, waiting anxiously for the results.

"We got a hit on one near the Tower of London," Alex said. "We had patrolmen already stationed there. Another one just pinged near the Millennium Wheel. And one more near Buckingham Palace, all places were guarded. But that's it."

"That's only three locations," Hawk said. "There's one more."

"I know, but we're not getting anything. Must be a call to someone else."

The pecking sound from Alex pounding on her keyboard came through the coms loud and clear.

"Do me a favor," Hawk said. "Crosscheck that number with Evana Bahar's number. Find out her last known location."

A half-minute elapsed before Alex responded. "Nothing. It's not pinging even close to her location."

"What else are we forgetting then?"

"Wait a minute," Alex said. "I just got something from that fourth number. It's right near the Houses of Parliament."

"I know that London police has officers responding to the scene, but right now it's chaotic around here and difficult to get any information. We're all just trying to regain our bearings after losing power."

Hawk stood and stared across the bridge toward Parliament. "I'll make my way over there now and see what I can find."

Breaking into a light jog before turning into a full sprint, Hawk raced toward the Houses of Parliament only to be held up by an officer who had a gun trained on him at the end of Westminster Bridge.

"Drop your weapon," the officer commanded.

Hawk held his hands in the air and gently set the gun down on the ground. "I'm working with law enforcement to stop these terrorist attacks," Hawk said.

"Keep your hands where I can see them."

"Speak to your commanding officer and tell them that you have Brady Hawk in your sights. Listen to what they say."

The officer sneered as he followed Hawk's suggestion. With wide-eyes the policeman listened to the rebuke, which was so loud that Hawk heard it ten meters away.

"I told you," Hawk said as the officer ended his communication.

"I apologize for the mistake," he said, gesturing for Hawk to continue.

Hawk snatched his gun off the ground and resumed sprinting. As he rounded the corner, Alex's voice crackled again in his ear.

"We've got a problem, Hawk."

"What now?"

"At the other three locations, we've arrested a small crowd of men wearing what appeared to be fake suicide vests, just like the one Davenport was wearing."

"You mean—"

"Yeah, more psychological torture. But it makes sense now since Fazil was never the type to sacrifice himself for the cause."

"Since it was never really about the cause—only revenge."

"So, everyone here is leaning toward this being a stunt by Al Hasib to get British authorities to gun down innocent Muslim citizens and use it as a recruiting tool. Davenport was the only person Fazil really wanted dead."

"I'm not so sure I can go along with that notion based on what Fazil said when we were talking up on the Tower Bridge," Hawk said. "I got the distinct impression that he wanted to be the next person of Guy Faulks's lore in England. And we know what Guy Faulks intended to do to the Houses of Parliament."

Hawk heard a commotion behind him and stopped, turning around to watch a handful of officers corralling about ten men wearing dishdashas and walking suspiciously together toward Parliament. With his gaze bouncing between the north bank of the Thames and the fracas at the nearby intersection, Hawk waited until one of the officers ripped open robe after robe, checking the men.

An officer threw his hands in the air and started cursing. A transport wagon roared up to the scene, and the men were handcuffed before getting shoved into the back of the truck.

"Are you watching something near you?" Alex asked. "I think I see you on the feed."

"If you're looking at the feed of the intersection of Westminster Bridge Road and Parliament Square, that's me," Hawk said.

"Someone just said those guys are wearing fake vests as well," Alex reported. "But at least nobody is dead yet—and no building has been reduced to rubble."

"There's something about this that doesn't feel right," Hawk said.

Noticing someone else walking behind the crowd, Hawk craned his neck to get a better look.

A woman clothed in a hijab glided past the commotion and headed along the north bank of the Thames that ran alongside the Houses of Parliament. Hawk raced after her.

"Alex," Hawk said.

"I see her, too," Alex said.

"Have someone else check the other potential

targets," he said. "I've got a bad feeling about all this."

As Hawk chased after the woman, he breezed past the officers still wrangling with the fake bombers. One of the men depressed the button on his vest in hopes of activating an explosion. Nothing happened. Hawk couldn't tell if the men were more upset that they couldn't become martyrs or that they were getting arrested. Knowing Fazil like Hawk did, he figured the Al Hasib leader didn't even tell the men that they were wearing dummy suicide vests.

Hawk saw the genius in the plan, but there was still time to squash it.

But he had to hurry.

CHAPTER 32

THE WOMAN WALKED swiftly toward the Houses of Parliament, checking repeatedly over her shoulder. Hawk didn't want to spook her, but he needed to get closer. Whenever she faced forward, he broke into a sprint, slowing to a casual walk with his head down when she turned around. In less than a minute, he was close enough that she was within earshot.

"You don't have to do this," Hawk said.

The woman kept moving, refusing to turn around.

"I know you have a bomb," Hawk said.

She stopped and turned to face him.

"Then you should know to keep your distance." She resumed her quick pace.

Hawk thought the woman looked familiar, but he wasn't sure.

"Alex," Hawk said softly into his coms, "look for any woman near those sites wearing a hijab. The men were just a diversion so the women could sneak past."

"On it," she said.

Hawk maintained his pursuit, attempting another appeal to the woman. "Fazil is dead," Hawk said. "It's over."

The woman stopped again and glanced back over her shoulder, her eyes looking down. "You would say anything to get me to stop, wouldn't you?"

"It's true. I saw his dead body sprawled out on Westminster Bridge."

"Was it you that killed him?"

"It had to be done. He was never going to stop. But you can."

The woman turned to face him, tears streaming down her cheeks. "There's no turning back now. I have only one purpose."

Hawk shook his head. "That's not true. You still have time, don't you?"

She glanced at her watch. "Not much, maybe three more minutes before this bomb goes off. It's why you need to get away from me if you don't want to die, too."

"Do you want to die?"

The woman took a deep breath and slowly shook her head. "Not tonight. But I have no choice now."

"If you want out, maybe I can help."

"My brother was taken to Gitmo and has been there for two years," she said. "I just wanted to do something to fight back against these people who have kept him there. He never did anything."

"Why was he arrested?"

"He was a delivery man, dropping off a package at a compound that happened to be the headquarters for a terrorist cell. They rounded him up with all the others, refusing to listen to his story. He's still in prison today."

"That's not right," Hawk said. "Someone should've listened to his side of the story. But what you're doing isn't going to change any of that. You're going to throw your life away, maybe take some innocent people with you. Do you want to continue to perpetuate that kind of violence?"

She shook her head. "Can you get this vest off me?"

"I can try," Hawk said as he rushed toward her. "You're the secretary from ROARS, aren't you?"

She nodded.

"What's your name?"

"Badia," she said. She shed her hijab and outer garment, revealing a vest attached to her midsection. The countdown showed he had just over a minute remaining.

"Alex, I need your help now," Hawk said as he knelt in front of the woman.

"What is it?" Alex asked.

"I need to remove one of these vests. Got any

ideas on how I can do that?"

"There's nothing you can do."

"What do you mean?"

"Fazil designed all his suicide vests to make sure no one chickened out. He obviously didn't trust anyone. The only way to turn those vests off is by some remote device. If you try to take it off, it detonates. No getting around it."

"What about this remote device?" Hawk asked. "Any idea where it's at?"

"You don't have time, Hawk."

Hawk sighed and looked up at Badia. "There's nothing I can do."

"Well, there's still time for me to do something."

Hawk glanced at the digital display. Fifteen seconds remained.

Badia sprinted toward the water, jumped up onto the short wall at the edge, and dove headfirst.

She disappeared beneath the murky Thames before a bright flash preceded an explosion. Water spewed into the air. The ground shook, setting off car alarms everywhere.

In the distance, Hawk heard three more explosions within seconds of one another.

"Talk to me, Alex," Hawk said. "What's happening? It sounds like London is under siege."

"It is."

CHAPTER 33

HAWK SPRINTED BACK toward the intersection where the London police officers were arresting the gang of men wearing dummy vests. They were all secured inside a large transport truck, guarded by a pair of officers.

"What happened over there?" one of the officers asked.

"These guys were a distraction," Hawk said. "The real bomber was a woman, but she's gone now."

"Her vest exploded?"

Hawk nodded.

"What a coward," the officer sneered.

"Actually, that couldn't be any further from the truth. She abandoned her mission and dove into the river to make sure no one else died."

"A coward who didn't even have the courage to finish her job."

Hawk knew he wouldn't get anywhere with the officer. "Keep this bridge blocked off. We need to make sure there aren't any more attackers."

"Who are you again?"

"Brady Hawk. Check with your commanding officer if you want to know more."

Hawk didn't wait around to see if they were going to take any action. He headed straight for Evana Bahar's apartment.

"We missed it," Hawk said to Alex. "This whole time, Evana was the real key to everything. She was the one who recruited all the people here."

"I did some digging on her earlier," Alex said. "Turns out she was at the same family wedding Fazil was when the drone obliterated the area. Her mother and sister were killed during the attack. Evana had the same motive for joining the nebulous cause of jihad as Fazil had."

"Through her job, she had access to Muslims who were easy targets," Hawk said. "Radicalizing them wasn't hard once they discovered the west's animosity toward Muslims."

"Now those people are dead, and she's getting away scot-free."

"For now, maybe, but we'll ferret her out one way or another," Hawk said. "I'm going to go check out her apartment before the London police go over and properly collect evidence."

"You sure that's a good idea right now?" Alex asked.

"Do you have any better ones? I think we need to get what we can get that will help us get a head start on her whereabouts. This might seem like a single event, but I can promise you that once she realizes there is a void in the leadership of Al Hasib, she will try to fill it."

"It'll start all over again, won't it?"

"Cockroaches and terrorists," Hawk said. "No matter how many you exterminate, they always come back."

"Still better to have to deal with only the occasional one than an infestation, right?"

"Absolutely. Let Spiller and Riley know what I'm doing," he said. "Any word on Davenport?"

"Not yet. I know he's supposed to be here soon. They stopped by the hospital first to take care of some of his injuries."

"Good," Hawk said. "He needed some serious medical attention after the torture he looked like he endured."

There was a pause as Hawk continued along his route to Evana's apartment.

"You haven't said anything yet about finally killing Fazil," Alex said, breaking the silence.

"What's there to say? The bastard is dead, though I doubt that means Al Hasib is going to disappear. They have a vast network all over the world, capable of penetrating even places we once considered safe."

"At least eliminating Fazil should set them back for a while. Losing a charismatic leader isn't easy to overcome."

"Like cockroaches, I'm sure they'll find a way to climb out of the rubble. But I'm not concerned with that right now. Evana is still a major threat, wherever she is."

"Where are you now?" Alex asked.

Hawk reported the nearest cross streets.

"Two more blocks and you'll be there," Alex said. "She's on the twelfth floor. Apartment number twelve forty-seven."

Hawk continued his brisk pace until he reached the front entrance. A London police officer stood outside the doors.

"What's going on, officer?" Hawk asked.

"I need you to stay outside right now," the officer answered. "We're conducting a sweep of the building and need to keep everyone out, including residents, until we're finished."

"Does this have to do with Evana Bahar?" Hawk asked.

The officer scowled and eyed Hawk cautiously. "Who are you?"

"Brady Hawk, and I've been working with the Ministry of Defense to stop this attack."

The officer shook his head. "Guess you weren't much help. The Tower of London suffered tremendous damage, and three people were killed by the debris. The gates of Buckingham Palace are gone, along with several members of the Queen's Guard and a half dozen civilians."

"It could've been much worse. Davenport isn't dead."

"I swear that man has nine lives. I thought he already used them all."

"Sometimes people will surprise you."

"Well, I don't care who you are. You're not getting into this apartment until the sweep is finished."

Before Hawk could say anything else, an explosion rocked the building. Shards of glass tinkled as they hit the sidewalk and street. Fiery debris fell from the twelfth floor, denting the pavement and vehicles parked against the curb.

"What was that?" Alex asked.

"Evana's apartment," Hawk said. "It just exploded."

"Why weren't you in there?"

"London PD was making a sweep of the building and prevented anyone from entering."

"And you just complied? That doesn't sound like you," Alex said.

"I've had enough for one night. But now I'm glad

I didn't get here first."

"She probably booby-trapped her apartment. One last jab at the authorities. She's got to be long gone by now."

"There's nothing for me here," Hawk said. "I'm heading to you now."

* * *

WHEN HAWK ARRIVED back at Whitehall a half hour later, the personnel still seemed on edge. Aides were scuttling documents back and forth between the decision makers. Analysts rifled through documents in search of clues. Directors with dour faces huddled together to discuss strategy.

Meanwhile, Blunt sat in the back of the room, taking in the chaos with a glass of scotch in one hand and a chewed cigar in the other. Hawk settled into a chair next to Blunt.

"If you're looking for the latest update, you might want to check with your fiancée," Blunt said with a wink.

"What have you been doing back here?" Hawk asked.

"Contemplating my retirement."

"All this excitement tonight wasn't enough to move the needle for you?"

"I think my adrenals were exhausted long ago," Blunt said as he stared at the frenetic scene in front of him. "I've had my share of running for my life. I want to put those days behind me as quickly as possible while I still have some time left on this planet."

"This planet is a better place because of you."

"Those are kind sentiments, but I'm not sure that's factually true. More people may be alive because of my work, but that doesn't always equate to making somewhere a better place. You, on the other hand, have done exactly what I hoped you would do."

"And what's that?"

"Take your missions seriously and handle every situation with justice and nobility. Nobody can look at the way you've acted in the heat of the moment and question your loyalty or your commitment to bringing justice to bear."

"Maybe I should've been a lawyer," Hawk said.

"You would've been bored in less than a month. I don't think you'd enjoy dealing with petty people and tenacious bullies all day long. Besides, you'd hate to wait for a gavel to drop for justice to occur."

Hawk nodded and pursed his lips. "You're probably right. This is more my speed."

"Well, for you and Alex there is still plenty of work to be done."

"We're a team," Hawk said. "We're Firestorm. Without you, we're just an operative and a handler."

"There were others, you know," Blunt said.

Hawk cocked his head to one side and furrowed his brow. "Others?"

"Firestorm wasn't just about you, though you are the best the agency has to offer."

"There are other Firestorm teams out there?"

Blunt took a deep breath and exhaled slowly. "I don't tell you everything for a reason. Sometimes you need to be protected so you can simply do your job."

"It's important to have as much information as possible to make the best decisions."

Blunt shrugged. "I doubt you would've done anything else differently had you known more. You've acted exemplary thus far, and I intend to let President Young know all about it."

"Who are the others?" Hawk persisted.

"You killed one of my rogue agents, but there's another team out there," Blunt said. "They only operate when you are preoccupied."

"And they're part of Firestorm?"

"Technically, they are their own black ops program as well-known as Titan. But your paths have never crossed."

"And you run this team as well?"

"More or less. It's why I'm in Europe so much. That's where they operate most, snuffing out organized crime syndicates. Same as you, just a different type of warfare. More cloak and dagger stuff than you're used to. But I don't want to talk about this any more. I want to sit here and watch these people come to the realization that the Firestorm team is why the entire city isn't ablaze right now and that their Secretary of Defense is still alive."

The doors flew open, and in walked Davenport. Analysts and aides swarmed him. He shooed them away and implored them to get back to work, telling them that there would be time for a reunion later.

"These folks love that man," Hawk said.

"As they should," Blunt said. "He's one of the really good guys in this field, though he may not be long for it now after what happened with Evelyn. She was such a sweet woman."

"You think he'll get out to protect his kids?"

"I think he'll realize his kids will never be safe no matter what he does. But if I were him, I'd retire somewhere remote and spend the rest of my days enjoying the family I have."

Hawk nodded. "Maybe he'll stick around then and fight for them."

"You never know how a person will handle tragedy like this, but whatever decision he makes, it'll probably be the right one for him. His next move will define him for the rest of his life."

Hawk watched Davenport's movement across the room with interest. When they locked eyes,

Davenport turned and strode directly toward Hawk.

Hawk stood and offered his hand. Davenport grabbed Hawk and gave him a hug.

"You saved my life," Davenport said. "I can never repay you for that."

"Just doing what you asked me to come here and do—help catch Karif Fazil."

Davenport withdrew and wagged his index finger. "Jumping off the Tower Bridge to save me didn't have anything to do with Fazil."

"I beg to differ," Hawk said. "That was our little mind game with him."

"How so?"

"Fazil had been torturing you psychologically. He was counting on you never leaving the Tower Bridge alive, but he wanted you to see what he was going to do to London. By being there, I pressed him into doing something he didn't want to do. He wanted to watch the culmination of his all his work all while avenging the death of his brother, a death he held you responsible for. But when you were gone, he decided—as he always does—that his cause wasn't worth dying for."

"But he still died in the end, thanks to you."

Hawk nodded. "He did, but not without a fight and not without taking some more innocent people with him."

"You did good, Mr. Hawk. And I'm not talking about just saving my life. This could've been London's 9/11 moment if you hadn't taken action. There's really no telling what else Al Hasib had in store or may still have in store for us."

"You're right," Hawk said. "There still may be more to come. But at least you can go home tonight to your children and be there for them in the morning when they wake up."

"I'm headed to the country where they're staying as soon as I get debriefed on what happened tonight."

Davenport turned to Blunt, who stood up. The two men shook hands.

"I'm deeply indebted to you and your team, Senator," Davenport said.

Blunt shook his head. "It's what allies do for one another. I'm just glad we could help."

Hawk watched Davenport walk away. Proud and resolute, he continued glad-handing all the team members who approached him.

"He's gonna be all right no matter what he decides to do," Hawk said. "That much, I'm sure of."

"I agree," Blunt said. "Now, go get Alex, and let's get the hell outta here."

CHAPTER 34

Washington, D.C.

HAWK FIDDLED WITH his blond wig before re-adjusting his sunglasses. Paying with cash, he bought a latte, one of his least favorite drinks. He eased into the booth across from *The Washington Post* reporter Camille Youngblood. Proceeding cautiously, he attempted to do everything in a manner that wasn't his style, even using his left hand at every opportunity. He wanted to make sure that nothing he did could ever be traced back to him, anecdotally or otherwise.

Camille stared at her notes before looking up and offering her hand.

"I appreciate you meeting with me today, Mr.—"

"Livingston," Hawk said. "Just call me Livingston."

"Okay, Mr. Livingston," she began, "I have a few questions for you about your involvement in Project Z."

"Alleged involvement," he corrected.

"All right, alleged involvement."

"I'll answer what I can as truthfully as possible," he said. "But I can't make any guarantees."

"What can you tell me about Firestorm?"

A faint smile flickered on Hawk's face. "I thought this was an interview, not a mining expedition. Ask me pointed questions or else this meeting won't last long."

She sighed. "Fine. How long have you been a part of Firestorm?"

"Since its inception."

"Which is how long?"

"You tell me."

Camille tapped her pen on her notebook. "Look, I'm trying to wrap my head around what's been going on with this program, and I'm not going to be able to do that if you continue to give me nebulous answers."

"You're the one who said that you knew about the program and wanted to expose it. I said I would talk, which to me means that I'll answer questions about my involvement in certain operations, not give you all the information carte blanche."

"If that's how you want this to go, fine," she said. "Let's start with this question. For your job, do you have to answer to J.D. Blunt, the former Texas senator?"

"Most of the time."

"Is Firestorm also known as Project Z?"

"I've only known what I do to be called Fire-storm. I can't confirm or deny that for you."

"Was your outfit involved in any recent attacks on U.S. soil?"

"A few."

"The attack on the Golden Gate Bridge a couple years ago?"

Hawk nodded.

"The incident at Washington Nationals Park last year?"

"Yes."

"The dirty nuke attack that was foiled?"

"We played a role in that as well."

"And this foiled plan in London?"

"Firestorm as well."

"That's quite an impressive list."

Hawk nodded subtly. "It is, but it's only able to happen because people don't know about it. The way we operate could be misconstrued as acting outside the law. And some people seem to have a problem with that."

"If we don't have the law, what do we have?"

"Sometimes the law causes chaos. Our legal system is so complex and expensive that justice isn't always a given, even though it should be. Sometimes we need to handle things differently."

Camille glanced at her notes. "Like wiretaps,

invasion of privacy, spying on U.S. citizens?"

"I know where you're going with this, and I have to say that you're veering far away from the point. The point of what we do is to try and keep the citizens of this country—and sometimes the citizens of our allies—safe from attack. If we required legal channels to apprehend these terrorists or thwart their attacks, this country would be a smoldering ash heap by now. If we gather information on people, it's only because they are suspected to be assisting a terrorist organization. There's nothing nefarious going on with how we handle each mission."

"What are you trying to say?"

Hawk sighed. "If you write about Firestorm, you're going to have special interest groups—the kind who claim to be bipartisan but are nothing but paid shills for one party or another—who feel they have to fight something they'll deem as evil and pressure Senators and members of Congress to do things that actually aren't in the best interest of this country. In other words, such an exposé could weaken our ability to defend this country. Imagine two months from now writing about the deadly attack that left a million people dead in New York City, all while knowing your article is what paved the way for Al Hasib or some other organization to carry out such atrocities."

Camille leaned back and set her pen down.

"People need to know about this. Unsuspecting Americans could have their privacy invaded and their freedoms trampled."

Hawk took a sip of his drink and set it down gently on the table.

"Let's go along with your theory for a moment that Firestorm is out there invading the privacy of hard-working, flag-waving Americans in between thwarting terrorist attacks. Simply by me being here, I am proving your supposition wrong. I could've checked your background and found a pressure point, something to get you to back off. But I didn't. I came here to meet you at the request of Senator Blunt. He thought I could simply persuade you to drop this story for the good of the American people, for the security of this country."

"There's no denying that what you've done is nothing short of amazing. I'm certainly not against my freedoms being protected. And from what you've told me, it seems like your team operates with great integrity. But what I'm concerned with is what if someone else heads the program and isn't quite as noble acting as Blunt has been. What if someone wants to use Firestorm to spy on their political foes or gain leverage over others? What then?"

"That's why we're shutting the program down," Hawk said. "Firestorm will cease to exist effective

264 | R.J. PATTERSON

tomorrow. No more missions. No more unfettered access."

"And no more protecting us from terrorists?"

Hawk shrugged. "I'm sure someone will come up with a new way to handle the relentless forces that try to strike against our country. It just won't be Firestorm."

"And what about you, Mr. Livingston? What will you do?"

"I don't know yet, but I do know that I've done a serviceable job in preventing disasters both at home and abroad. And most importantly, Karif Fazil is dead."

"Did you kill him?"

"If you're asking if I fired the trigger, yes. If you're asking why he's dead today, it has more to do with his unquenchable thirst for vengeance and his arrogance. He could've achieved what he wanted to in the dead of night, but he wanted the world to see. And instead, everyone witnessed his downfall."

"I appreciate your willingness to speak with me, but I still feel strongly about this story."

"Why?" Hawk asked. "You want to tell everyone that a government black ops program existed that saved thousands of Americans but is now defunct? That's not a story. That's history. And it's not much different than what people already know. Do you think anyone cares who stopped Al Hasib? Most Americans are smart enough to realize these things exist and they exist for a good reason. If you go stirring up a hornet's nest over this and turn this thing into a political football, no one will be better for it."

"People have a right to know what their government does."

Hawk shook his head slowly. "Trust me when I say this, what Firestorm did was far less than the liberties taken by other agencies. And, yes, I know that's a logical fallacy and doesn't make it right, per se. But in our case, the ends justified the means. No one's political career has been destroyed because of what Firestorm ever did. We only fought for what was best for this country and took that fight to wherever it was necessary, even the White House at times."

"This is a story that needs to be told."

"How about you tell a better one," Hawk suggested.

"Okay, Mr. Livingston. Do you have one for me?"

Hawk pursed his lips. "Only on the condition that you agree never to write about Firestorm again or mention it to anyone. Destroy your notes, delete the files, whatever you need to do to make sure the shadow organization stays in the shadows."

"How good of a story is this?" she asked.

"The inside scoop on how we took down Karif Fazil and saved London from an even worse disaster."

Camille took a deep breath and looked out the window. She exhaled slowly before turning her attention back to Hawk.

"Okay, I'll agree to your terms, mostly because I know if I don't, I might end up dead in an alley somewhere. And I'd rather *be able* to tell a story."

"Good choice," Hawk said with a reassuring smile. "You're gonna want to pick up your pen and take notes on this. It's a sordid tale of vengeance, pride, and human ingenuity and determination."

"Proceed," she said.

CHAPTER 35

J.D. BLUNT WAS THE lone witness at Hawk's and Alex's wedding in Hawaii. Blunt waited until after the ceremony to tell them what they already suspected was coming: his official retirement announcement.

"I'm not leaving this island until I've bought a boat either," Blunt said.

"I didn't realize just how serious you were about that," Alex said.

"Dead serious," Blunt said. "Only this time, I'll have quite an arsenal with me in case someone decides to attack me out on the open water. But I'm hoping for a more peaceful sailing adventure."

"Well, if anyone has earned it, you have," Hawk said. "And I can't tell you how much I've appreciated our friendship over the years, especially our time together at Firestorm. You've been like a father to me. I mean, you've been like what I *think* a father should be like."

Blunt shrugged. "It comes with the territory.

You're one hell of an operative, Hawk. And, Alex, there's not a finer handler and analyst in any government agency on the planet. The CIA was foolish for letting petty politics get in the way of keeping you on."

"Thank you, sir," Alex said. "That means a lot coming from you."

"Well, thank you for your loyalty and service. And best of luck in whatever you two decide to do next."

Blunt reached into his coat pocket and dug out a cigar before jamming it into his mouth.

"One more thing before I leave," Blunt said. "I got you two a little something, though Hawk may appreciate this gift a bit more."

He sauntered over to a nearby table and scooped up a package wrapped in wedding paper. Handing the package to Hawk, he beamed while watching the couple unwrap the gift.

Hawk reached inside the box and pulled out a bottle. "Glenmorangie Pride 1974."

Alex gasped. "You shouldn't have."

Hawk shook his head. "This old codger has been trying to get me to come around to his scotch drinking ways ever since we started working together. He knows I'm more of a whisky drinker."

"But this is Glenmorangie Pride 1974," Alex said, the pitch in her voice rising with each word. "It's super expensive."

"And delicious," Blunt said as he put his hat on. "Enjoy."

He walked out of the room with a smile on his face and a little skip in his step.

* * *

THREE MONTHS LATER, Hawk and Alex were settling onto the couch for a Bollywood movie marathon when the phone rang.

"Should I answer it?" Hawk asked.

"Who is it?"

"Unknown number."

"Why not? You know I hate unsolved mysteries."

Hawk smiled. "Whatever you say, dear. But don't blame me if it's bad news."

"Why would it be bad—"

"This is Hawk," he answered.

"I was hoping you'd pick up," Blunt said.

Seagulls squawked in the background and along with intermittent gusts of wind, making it difficult to hear everything Blunt was saying.

"You're gonna have to repeat that," Hawk said. "I assume you're at port somewhere."

"Yes, yes," Blunt said. "Let me get down below deck." A few seconds later, they continued their conversation.

"Did you call to check on how married life was going?" Hawk asked.

"How'd you know?"

"Where are you right now?"

"I can't really tell you for sure, but let's just say it's nice and sunny here and the beer is cold."

"What about the scotch?" Hawk asked.

"There's still work to do in that area, but I have my own stash for emergencies."

"So, what's really going on?"

"I have an assignment for you, one that requires your immediate attention," Blunt said.

"An assignment?" Hawk asked, furrowing his brow. "What are you talking about? Firestorm is no more, though I did read in *The Washington Post* about a U.S. operative who foiled a terrorist attack in London."

"That was a nice article. But you know our work is never done."

"You aren't really retired, are you?"

"I'm about as retired as you are single these days."

"So, what's this assignment?" Hawk asked.

"The CIA needs some stuff handled off book. I can't really talk about this on the phone, but if you're willing to come back and work on this—"

"Is this just for me or both of us?"

"Both of you, of course. I wouldn't dare think of splitting up my dream team."

"Hold on a second and let me ask Alex what she

thinks." Hawk glanced at Alex and covered the phone. "Blunt has an assignment for us if we want it. Are you in?"

Alex's eyes lit up, and she nodded.

Hawk uncovered the phone and took a deep breath. "We're in."

THE END

ACKNOWLEDGMENTS

I am grateful to so many people who have helped with the creation of this project and the entire Brady Hawk series.

Krystal Wade was a big help in editing this book as always.

Also, I have to thank Sean Chuma from Inter-Demented BASE in Twin Falls, Idaho, for helping me answer some tough questions about BASE jumping as it related to the final climactic scene in the book.

I would also like to thank my advance reader team for all their input in improving this book along with all the other readers who have enthusiastically embraced the story of Brady Hawk. Stay tuned ... there's more Brady Hawk coming soon.

ABOUT THE AUTHOR

R.J. PATTERSON is an award-winning writer living in southeastern Idaho. He first began his illustrious writing career as a sports journalist, recording his exploits on the soccer fields in England as a young boy. Then when his father told him that people would pay him to watch sports if he would write about what he saw, he went all in. He landed his first writing job at age 15 as a sports writer for a daily newspaper in Orangeburg, S.C. He later attended earned a degree in newspaper journalism from the University of Georgia, where he took a job covering high school sports for the award-winning *Athens Banner-Herald* and *Daily News*.

He later became the sports editor of *The Valdosta Daily Times* before working in the magazine world as an editor and freelance journalist. He has won numerous writing awards, including a national award for his investigative reporting on a sordid tale surrounding an NCAA investigation over the University of Georgia football program.

R.J. enjoys the great outdoors of the Northwest while living there with his wife and four children. He still follows sports closely. He also loves connecting with readers and would love to hear from you. To stay updated about future projects, connect with him over Facebook or on the inter-webs at www.RJPbooks.com and sign up for his newsletter to get deals and updates.

Made in the USA
Monee, IL
23 May 2022

96906121R00162